The Last Girls On Earth

Book 2: Gluttony

HAYLEY ANDERTON

This book is dedicated to the girls on Bookstagram. The ones who I've never met in real life, but who support me so unconditionally anyway. I love you all.

OTHER BOOKS BY HAYLEY ANDERTON

All books are available to purchase as paperbacks or ebooks.
All books are also enrolled in Kindle Unlimited.

The Last Girls on Earth

Book 1: Sloth
Book 2: Gluttony
Book 3: Greed

Apocalypse Series

Book 1: Apocalypse
Book 2: Fallout
Book 3: Chaos
Book 4: Sacrifice
Book 5: Outlast
Book 6: Alliance

Coming Soon…
The Risen Series

Book 1: The Risen
Book 2: The Lost
Book 3: The Remains

Other Books:

Double Bluff
Homebound

What isn’t yours you hope to claim,
You clasp lone scraps with shame,
A mouth starved never tires
Of a hungry heart's wildest desires.

RILEY

My head hurts like a bitch.

It's my first thought as I pry open my eyes and look up. I can feel cool air brushing my cheeks, and I can see the sky. Am I still in the Pit? Have I woken up with Bull's blood on my hands? Guilt sears through my heart like an ice pick.

But then I realize I'm moving. Someone, or something, is carrying me, and they're not doing a very good job. I'm bouncing around all over the place on some kind of stretcher. I try to sit up instinctively, but a wave of nausea sends me shooting backward. As my shoulder hits the stretcher, pain bursts through me. Whoever is carrying me yelps and loses their balance, toppling us to the ground.

"Bloody hell!" I cry out as my spine jolts on the tarmac. I blink through the pain. We seem to be in some dark alleyway in a city that seems unfamiliar to me. Away from the Pits, then. "What the hell is going on here?"

"Sleeping Beauty awakes,' Squid grins, his dopey face hovering over mine. "About bloody time too, if you ask me. I was starting to think you'd joined the land of the dead."

I blink through the bleariness of my eyes, and three faces come into focus. Looking down on me are people I thought I might never see again. Pup's eyes are filled with worry, while

Tiger seems relieved and Squid has a huge grin on his face.

"Don't joke about that," Pup whispers. "It's too soon."

"Agreed," Tiger says with a disapproving sniff. "We've just lost two. Pup's all beat up-"

"It's Elianna," she says softly. "We don't need those nicknames anymore."

"In any case...Elianna is beat up, and-"

"-Riley can't even walk by herself," Elianna finishes for him. "So no more jokes about death, okay? It's just not funny."

Squid raises an eyebrow at me. "Well, there you have it. No room for jokes. You two are just a barrel of laughs, aren't you?" Squid pauses, prodding me with his finger. I wince. Every single inch of me feels sore. "Well, say something, eh? Cat finally got your tongue?"

I huff.

"Fuck off."

"There she is…"

"Does someone mind telling me what the hell is going on?"

"You're on the road, kid," Squid says. "We left the Pit behind three days ago. We wanted to stay longer, let you and Pup recover…"

"It's *Elianna.*"

"...but they closed down the ward. Lion was practically shoving us out the door. I guess she's moving on to bigger and better things."

I take a few deep breaths, forcing my body to start thinking for itself again. Three days…that means I've been out for at least that long. Given how badly I got beaten up, it must be longer than that since I was last conscious. But that means it's been at least that long since I ended Bull's life. A chill runs down my spine. How could I be capable of what I did? Am I really that desperate to live that I would kill one of my own?

Apparently so.

The pain of my guilt hurts worse than the ache in my jaw

and the blow to my nose. Worse than the throbbing in my back that I can feel now. Much worse than the place where the knife entered my shoulder and the slashes across my face. And I know this is the kind of wound you can't patch up with some bandages. I clutch my stomach. I feel like I might throw up.

"The world is spinning."

"Lie back down," Elianna says, trying to help me, but I shrug her off. I'm not in the mood for her to act like nothing happened between us back at the Pits. *Sometimes I think you don't have a damn heart.* That's what she told me. Well, if she wants me to act heartless, I can manage that just fine where she's concerned.

I shift into a more comfortable position on the ground and the others ditch the stretcher to sit with me. We're quiet now, not knowing what to say to one another. This alleyway smells of piss and it's making my headache worse. Elianna fishes in her bag and produces some slightly moldy looking bread.

"Are you hungry? You must be?" she says gently. I narrow my eyes at her. What, does she think now that I almost died, now that I had to kill one of our own, that I've been punished enough for coming up with the idea of the fight in the first place? Pfft. She wouldn't have made it this far if I hadn't done that. Even if she was the one carrying me and not the other way around, she's alive because of me. They all are. I made the sacrifice so that they didn't have to.

I snatch the bread from her hands and gnaw at it, picking away the moldy parts. Then I realize just how hungry I am and scarf those bits too. I need to remember my roots. I'm not above eating something past its best. Staying at the Pits made me soft, clearly.

"Better?" Elianna asks me when I'm done, but I ignore her. I'm not done being mad at her yet. Like she can give the silent treatment and I can't do it to her? That's just typical Elianna. She does everything on her own terms. I stare at the ground, my whole body hurting and my heart squeezing hard every time I think about what I had to do. I guess when I was out of it, I was granted some peace for a bit. Now all I can see is Bull's face in my mind as she died in my arms.

"Cheer up, kiddo," Squid says. "We've got a big wad of cash in our bags and the world is our oyster. Life isn't so bad."

"Is that so?" Elianna says coldly. "So that's why we're wandering around aimlessly, trying to avoid government officials, is it? Pretending like we're not going to get in trouble the moment we're found without ID? You know they'll shoot us on sight."

Squid sighed. "Come on, princess, you know they're not looking at us. Don't you think the police have enough going on right now?"

Elianna scowls at Squid. "Princess?"

"Well, you said you didn't like Pup anymore…"

"My name is Elianna. You know that."

Squid catches my eye with a grin. "Alright then, Princess."

I smirk. Normally, I'm the one sticking up for Elianna, but I'm not in the mood for that today. Besides, a little teasing from Squid won't do her any harm. In fact, it's cheered me up a little. I forgot how easily Squid can lift my mood. Elianna might be my oldest friend, but Squid has always been the big brother that I've spent my life wishing for. He's kept me under his wing for a long time. When I arrived at the Pits, he was the one who showed me the ropes, trained me up, made sure I didn't end up dead. How is it possible that I was thinking about leaving him behind, going my own way?

This is why, I remind myself, *because you get too damn attached.*

"Do we have a plan?" I ask, pushing my thoughts aside. I don't want to get caught up in them now. I know that I need all three of them right now to stay alive. I'm in no fit state to go it alone. If I have to stay with my friends until I'm better, then so be it. That's how we survive, right?

"No plan," Squid says with a grin. "We're going with the flow."

"What about getting to your family?" I ask. I know he had plans to go and find his mum. Why would he change his mind?

Squid ruffles my shorn hair gently, sending a throbbing sensation through my aching head. "And what about this family, huh? I can't leave you like this, little tyke. When you're better we'll go together."

I press my lips together. I don't know what to tell him. I want to ask him what's the point? What's the point when soon enough, we'll all wind up dead? Even with my eyes open, I see Bull's face behind my eyes as she lay dead on the ground. I don't know why I didn't just let her kill me then. She near enough did, and now what am I going to do? Keep fighting like this forever just to stay alive?

Will we ever know what it's like to sleep in a bed again? Will we ever know what it's like to feel warm, to have new boots to cover our feet, to feel hot food inside our bellies? Will I ever be able to scrub the dirt from my skin, brush my teeth, find new clothes to cover my scars? Or is this it now? Trying not to die on the road, stinking to high heaven, surrounded by a bunch of other murderers?

Some life this is.

"I don't like this," Tiger says quietly. There's a smudge of dirt across his pale, freckled cheek. I know from the Pits how much Tiger values keeping clean, and this must be killing him, out here in the dust and dirt. His hands are quaking on his knees. "I don't want to be out here. I don't know how to be this way anymore."

There's silence between us, and Elianna nods, but says nothing. We let his comment hang in the air like a rotten fruit hanging from a tree. Nobody wants to be the one to pluck it, but someone's got to.

"How much were the spoils?" I whisper.

"Three grand," Elianna says quietly. I wince. Now I know the price of Bull's death. Nice to put a number on my blood money, I guess.

"Not enough to buy us the X drug," I mutter. Elianna

and Tiger exchange a look and I latch on to their exchange. "What? What are you looking like that for?"

"Well…we talked about it," Elianna says. "And actually, it is. It's enough to buy it for you."

I scowl at her, still not done being mad at her. "What the hell are you talking about?"

"You won the fight, Riley. It was your idea to fight in the first place," Tiger tells me. "So we think that it should be yours to do as you please."

"If it buys one of us freedom and life…then it's for a good cause," Elianna says. "You should take it. What was the point of fighting if you won't get to live?"

She's got a point. I've been thinking the same myself. But I'm not that damn selfish. If I could have all the money in the world in exchange for leaving my friends alone with nothing, I wouldn't take it. Street rats stick with street rats, and that's final. I've got nothing if I haven't got some morals.

"No. I'm not taking it," I tell them firmly. "We're going to find a way to make more of it."

"Like get a job? Another fighting pit?" Tiger asks. Squid cracks his knuckles.

"Bring it on. I'm ready for anything."

"No, not the Pits. Not again," I say. I don't think I could do it again even for all the money in the world. Fighting Bull broke me. I have to do something now that'll save what's left of us, to redeem myself for what I did. "There are better ways to make money."

"There are?" Squid says, raising an eyebrow. My lips twist into a sort of smile. The closest I'm going to get to smiling right now when I feel so shitty. But there's an old calling screaming out to me right now. Dragging me home.

"Do any of you know how to play cards?"

RAVEN

I wake with a stiff back and an empty stomach. My body creaks as I sit up and stretch. I blink several times. It takes longer than usual for the world to come into focus.

We're in the headmaster's old office at Logan's school. It's larger than the entire apartment my family used to own. There are two couches – one of which Jonah has taken. Logan and I have been taking it in turns to sleep on the floor. Last night was my turn. I try not to groan as I stand up. No use in complaining. It's not much worse than the life I'm used to.

It's been twenty three days since the government announced their plans to turn our country upside down. To round up the poor and have them killed so that the rich can live without guilt. And to top it all off, they'll live with the X drug shot up in their veins, making them closer to Gods than humans. But some of the rest of us aren't ready to bow down and take it yet. I'm certainly not. Maybe if I was alone, I'd feel differently. But I have my brother to fight for. Logan and his friends too. Somewhere out there, Wren might even still be alive. There's a future out there for us all if we're willing to find it, I just know it. Our lives may be small and insignificant, but I'm determined that someday, somewhere, we will matter.

It's time to start the day. I peer over at Jonah's sleeping form with a smile. In his sleep, he looks relaxed, even after everything he's been through. Logan, on the other hand, sleeps stiff on the other sofa, flat on his back with an arm over his eyes like he's shielding himself from the world. I move to wake him up with a shake and he sighs, tossing on the sofa so his back is to me. I jab a finger in his ribs and he jumps to life. I grin as he sits up, scowling.

"Rise and shine," I whisper. I don't want to wake Jonah. "Are you feeling sunny and motivated this morning?"

"Like hell I am," he mutters. I smile. He's not used to running on empty like the rest of us. I offer him a hand and help him up, my body aching with the effort. Logan sighs, wiping sleep from his eyes.

"What's on the agenda today?" I ask.

Logan produces a clipboard from the table behind him. He scans the page, his eyes trying twice as hard to focus as normal. "We are going on a food run. Hopefully this time we'll get a good haul."

"I've told you where we need to go. The black market storeroom will be stocked to the max."

"And also guarded to the max," Logan reminds me. We've been having this argument all week. "The only way we'll get supplies off them is if we buy it, and we don't have that kind of money anymore. They've hiked the prices up, for sure. If we go in there, guns blazing, we'll all be killed. The black market isn't an option."

"So where do you plan to take us instead?"

"It's not up to me. Ellis is running this expedition. She'll let us know in the brief."

I almost roll my eyes. Ellis might think she's capable of running the show, but she's not the brightest. Following her plans feels like a good way to end up dead. Still, she has power here and I don't. There doesn't seem much sense in trying to argue with her. And since she managed to pull this place together on a moment's notice, I should really give her more credit. We wouldn't have made it this far without what she's done for us.

I make sure Jonah's all tucked up in his blanket before leaving him to sleep on the couch. I don't like leaving him, but there's work to be done. At least I know he'll be safer here than anywhere else. Besides, if all goes well, I'll be back in a few hours, maybe with some food so he won't go hungry.

We take the stairs to the room where we've been holding all of our meetings. It's a large oblong space with a table that runs almost the entire length of it. The walls have black and white photography arranged in frames. I think they're pictures of how this place used to be, before it was left to ruin.

The longest wall is entirely made of glass and gives a view of the entire city. Looking down makes my knees wobble, but looking out over the rooftops is breathtaking. We've claimed some of the buildings nearest to us as our own, expanding our territory a little, and guards with guns stand atop them, keeping an eye on the quiet streets. Further in the distance, crowds of protestors still fight. There are fires burning night and day. They've not shown any signs of giving in, which I guess is good. Even though eventually, they'll lose. For a while, it keeps the attention off us. It's a selfish thought, but selfishness is what is most likely to keep us alive. While they're still fighting, we're left to build up our defenses and make a proper go of this life we're trying to create. I have no idea how long it'll be before it comes crashing down around us, but the worse things are out there, the better things look from in here.

But the main thing I've been looking for is signs of the people Kai and I saw on the bus. The crazed, mutated people who chased after us. So far, I've not seen any when I've been outside the perimeter. Sometimes in the night, I hear gunfire and know the guards have shot another one down. Rumor has it that a group of people within our walls have been examining the bodies, trying to figure out what happened to them, though it's difficult when no one knows what they're looking for. With the exception of Logan and a few others, everyone here is far from educated, let alone a science expert. But if these people are products of drugs A to W, I can only begin to imagine what the X drug does to people.

Logan stands next to me as I look out at the city. He looks sad, which takes me aback. I haven't really considered what he's losing. He was born into wealth and education and civility. To see the world falling apart outside must be odd to him. I'm better prepared – my life was never held together in the first place. It's harder for him to process this, I think. Perhaps privilege isn't always a good thing.

"I used to love reading the history of our country," he says. "I've always wondered how we got to how we are. It's so interesting, Raven. For hundreds of years, way before cities like this existed, Britain lived without electricity, without clean water, without machinery to make everything for us. And then there was a technology boom. Everybody had televisions. Everybody had cars."

"But how did everyone afford it?"

"At the time, these things weren't really considered a luxury to most people. It was almost like a right. And the population was smaller, so there was enough to go around. Electricity was used in abundance. It powered everything we did. People would carry around mobile phones and compact computers. We had endless access to the internet. Everybody used it to communicate when they were apart. They'd post pictures and videos and ramblings about life on social media websites. It was crazy." Logan shakes his head, wonderstruck. "And then we overwhelmed ourselves with it all. We became reliant on these new ways to survive. Polluted the Earth and cried when it fell apart. We expanded so much that the population on this silly little island became too much. And it created poverty, it created shortages, it created this mess. The government blamed immigration and the poorest people in the country, but everyone else knew better than to believe that. They were the ones who messed up. Now I look outside and realize how lucky I was to have even a fraction of those things. None of us will have that again in our lifetime."

"You think?"

Logan nods. He stares outside at the fire and the destruction. He nods again. "Everything is being destroyed. Even if they beat us down, if they get what they want out of this, the people left behind will be clearing up this mess for years. This war will cost them money. The economy will go crazy. Prices will inflate."

"In English, please."

"Everything will get more expensive because it's in high demand, with few resources. Basically, things will go to shit."

"You do realize that's how we've been living anyway? Our family couldn't afford a loaf of bread most days. I don't need fancy words to know that."

Logan looks down at his feet. "I'm sorry. I…sometimes I struggle to step out of my own shoes and see your perspective."

"You're trying, at least."

Logan sighs. "Well, I guess I'll learn quickly enough. Nothing will be normal ever again."

"Sounds like everyone's got plenty to look forward to."

Logan smiles. "I know it sounds crazy, but if we get through this…I think we'll be the happy ones. We'll never be part of the society they want to build. But we can go it alone. Find ways to feed ourselves. Make ourselves a home. Live outside the law."

I laugh out loud this time. "Listen to yourself, Logan. Romanticizing the life I've had all along. I've been *living outside the law* all my life. So has Jonah. So has everyone in this building. We never had a choice, and we never will. Do you think we were happy?"

Logan's smile droops. "No…no, I don't think so. I know it's never been easy, and it probably never will be. But maybe someday, it'll be better. And then I'll figure out how to put a smile on your face."

I wonder what he means by that. Before I can reply, the

door opens and people begin to flood in. The meeting's about to start. Logan looks like he wants to say something else, but I shrug at him and take a seat at the table. We don't have time to dream about the future when we're trying to survive the present.

There are about twenty people in the room. We're all people that the community trusts. That's why they chose us to lead. Since arriving, I've done my best to help however I can and to get to know people. It's the only reason I've been allowed to stay on what they're calling 'the council.' Ellis has grown less apprehensive towards me, but I can tell she still doesn't approve. Maybe she thinks I'm too young to be here, but I've survived this long without help. I'm sure I can offer this council *something*.

"So," Ellis says as soon as the last person has hit their seat. Everyone ceases their conversations right away. "We'll be covering a new section of town today. We've explored most of what's within a several mile radius of us, but there's one last place we can try." Ellis spreads a city map on the table and chairs creak as everyone leans in to take a closer look. Ellis points out the school on the map.

"North of us is the richest part of town. There's no doubt there will be things to gather from there. Logan has informed us of some hotspots, but we'll tackle those another day when we've explored a little and got a feel for the situation uptown. For now, our plan is to try and blend in. We'll dress like them and try to act like we belong up there. Logan, can you provide us with some clothing that will help?"

"I brought some with me from home, suitable for all genders. There's maybe five or six outfits."

"That'll be enough. The team is small today – we don't want to draw any attention to ourselves. We'll take minimum weapons. Only things that can be easily concealed. The target is here." Ellis points at the map again. It shows a large building on the high street. "This supermarket is sure to be well stocked. Take your time. Each fill a trolley with items. Then when it comes to leave, you'll have to run. As long as you're quick, you won't be caught. As far as we know, there aren't any police stationed there, so once you're away, you'll be okay."

I can't help laughing. Ellis glares at me and I shake my head. "I'm sorry. I can't help it. This is your plan? You can't be serious. Do you have any clue what we could be walking into? And with no weapons?"

Ellis stands up, as though to emphasize her annoyance. She glares at me. "We've been unable to send in scouts to check out the area. We can't just walk in with guns. The rich have the army backing them. We're doing our best with what we have."

"Your best isn't good enough," I say, standing up. Logan grabs my arm, trying to sit me back down.

"Raven…"

Ellis circles around the table to get to me. She jabs a finger in my chest. "Look here. We can always find another scout if you're not going. Or perhaps you have a better plan?"

"I'm sure I can whip something up," I say, snatching up the map. I examine it, looking for viable options – back alleys we could take or ways we could remain hidden. The map doesn't reveal much.

"Which side is the front of the shop?"

"The side that faces the shopping street," Ellis says. She pauses. "Obviously," she adds as a jab. I ignore it. I've got a plan forming.

"So…if we knew what time the delivery van arrived, we could potentially hijack it. It'll obviously go around the back where the storeroom is. All we'd have to do is wait until the drivers get out to unload it and then slip into the driver's seat. Some of the others can try and sneak out the back with supplies from in store."

"It's risky," Ellis argues.

"And running like a mad man for a mile with a trolley is a better one?" I shake my head. "I'm not doing that. If you kick me off the team, then fine. But I want to come back in one piece. I know there's risk in either idea, but if we got a delivery van, we'd not only gain the food, but transport."

June, who has been quiet up until now, clears her throat. "I think she's right, Ellis. You have to admit. Our idea was a little far-fetched."

Ellis' lips twist. Her forehead crumples. She moves away from me. "Fine. So I suppose you'll want to lead the team too?"

That's more than I bargained for. I'm not a leader, and I'd never want to be. But I can't back down now that I've shown Ellis up. I stand up straight. "Fine."

"Fine," Ellis repeats. "Pick your team."

I scan the room. I want people who are fast, strong, sly. And of course, I'm not going anywhere without Logan. I pat his shoulder to let him know and he nods. The rest of the choices won't be so easy. If I had it my way, I'd have Kai with me. His mind is as sharp as his tongue. He'd be an asset to our team. But I doubt June will let me take him. He's still just a kid, after all. So I'll have to pick more carefully.

"Valeria?" I ask, tentative. She's sitting half way down the table on her own. She's built like a tank, hair the color of blood. It's shorn at the sides to reveal a tattoo on her skull of a rose. She's hardly light on her feet, and nothing about her is subtle, but she's strong. She'll be useful in a fight. She shrugs at me.

"Okay," she says. "I can drive too. If that helps. For the getaway."

"It does," I say, glad to have made a good choice. Logan nudges my arm.

"I'd recommend taking Roger. He's pretty swift. He came on the last food run with me."

Logan nods across the table and a sturdy man opposite me stands up, offering a hand to shake. I take it and he smiles at me. I find myself smiling back. His face is inviting. Charming. Undeniably handsome. He's got dark hair and sharp cheekbones, with eyes so dark they're almost black. I don't know how I missed him when he was sitting right opposite me.

"I'd be happy to help," he says.

"Glad to hear it.'

"Two more," Logan reminds me. I do my best to look like I know what I'm doing as I scan the room. I don't know anyone here well enough to trust them on my team. Except two.

"June and Ellis. That will be enough," I say. Though Ellis and I don't get on, she's pretty quick. June's smart, and a good keeper of the peace. Exactly what I need. I nod, trying to look confident. I can feel everyone's eyes on me. I clear my throat.

"Right, then. Logan should get us kitted out. Then we'll pick up some weapons. Does anyone know how to use a gun?"

Valeria raises her hand and I nod to her. "Right. Good."

"Hang on a second. Guns?" Ellis hisses. "We can't."

"It's a precaution," I argue, "Just a small pistol will do. If we get in trouble, we can use it as a last resort. I'm not risking any of our lives and putting it down to chance. I trust that Valeria knows what she's doing."

Ellis shakes her head, but doesn't argue any further. Logan stands up and the others on our team follow suit. As we leave the room, I hear another member of the council bring up rationing.

I close the door behind me. My team watch me, expectant. I raise my chin. Confidence is key, I decide. None of them will trust my judgment if I splutter and stutter my way through the mission.

"Let's get started."

KARISSA

I'm alone in the bunk room, absentmindedly tying and re-tying my shoelaces. Each knot seems inadequate and I start over again. I need the conditions to be perfect today for Team Nine. Our afternoon will be taken up by Combat Training, and I need to figure out how to bring the team together before we enter the simulation.

Since I was chosen as Team Leader, things have not been going to plan. No one's talking to one another, which makes sense since our team was completely humiliated in front of everyone for breaking the rules. Everyone's mad at my brother and he's mad at everyone else. I'm sitting somewhere in the middle of this mess while people try and figure out how to feel about me, their new leader. It doesn't make a good team environment and I don't know how to resolve it. I'm not good at small talk – I don't know how to chat with these people. But I have to try now. They're my responsibility. If I can't pull us all together before we go into the field, then we'll all wind up dead.

I give up on my laces and go to meet the team outside the classroom. Elliott is stoic and silent, glaring at me as I join them in the queue for the simulation. Minnie has abandoned her usual red lips in favor of plain today. Even Zach, our usual class clown, isn't joking around. The attention is still on my brother. The resentment towards him hangs heavy in the air. I guess it should please me. Elliott has long been a thorn in my side, keeping the others out of favor with me. But I have to remind myself that it's not good to have schisms in the team, even if this is what I've hoped for for years. We have to work together to complete tasks such as the ones we'll face in Combat Training today. Which means I need to figure out quickly how to get everyone on the same side again.

"Okay, team," I say, trying to sound enthused. The team turn their glares on me. I swallow hard. I can't break character now.

"Okay, so, as we all know, this is one of the most important classes we take. It determines if we're ready to go into battle. I know we all want the same thing – we want to be out there with the top teams, rounding up and killing all the Inferiors. Am I right?"

Marcia and Ronan mutter something unintelligible in response. The others remain silent. I purse my lips. "Well, if we don't pull it together, we won't be one of those teams. This has to go well today. Which means working together. So here's how this is going to work. I'll lead whatever mission we are given. Zach, for the purpose of this task, I'd like you to act as my Second. The rest of you will fall behind us. You'll follow our orders. If you'd like to express an opinion, you'll first ask permission to speak. Am I clear?"

Zach snorts. "Damn, girl. You expect us just to fall in line with everything you say? We didn't pick you. We don't want you as our leader. You think you can just muscle your way in and expect us to like you?"

I grab Zach by his shirt. He gasps in surprise as I shake him a little. "Listen to me. If you want to be Second you'd better buck up. That's no way to speak to your Team Leader. I am not here to make you like me. I am here to be obeyed." I let go of him and Zach blinks, knocked stupid for a few seconds. I glare around the group. "I didn't choose to be leader, okay? This was dumped on me as much as it was dumped on you. But I have a job to do. As my team, you have to follow my orders, whether you like it or not. Don't make me dole out punishments. I want our team to function positively. Okay?"

They all remain unanimated. Minnie stares at her nails. Marcia hangs her head. I try not to show my annoyance. "I can't hear you," I say.

"Okay," Zach mutters, "Okay."

I roll my shoulders back. None of this feels right. But I can't back down now. I have to get everyone in place. "Okay. Let's do this."

A few minutes later, the doors to the simulation room open and we're allowed to go inside. At the door, we're handed a headset each for communication with Captain Strauss. Then we're each handed a knife and a gun. Of course, everything in this room is simulated - none of what we see or feel here will be real. The bullets we shoot will be fake, and the knife we're given is blunted. But it will feel like it's real, and this is to prepare us for the real world. There's no room for error in here.

The doors shut behind us and we're left in the dark. I hear a mechanical whirring as the room arranges itself for our mission.

"Team Nine. Welcome to Combat Training. I trust you've all settled with your new Team Leader," Captain Strauss says on the headset. I almost snort. Chance would be a fine thing.

"Your mission is relatively simple. There is a group of Inferiors loose in the city streets. Your job is to eliminate them. You will be outnumbered, so remember to consider your tactics before you throw yourself at them. The simulations will react accordingly to your actions. Remember – Combat Training will always present you with the worst-case scenario. If you can handle this, real battles will be a doddle. The Inferiors are no match for you all – especially if you have the element of surprise. Good luck to you! Let's see what you're all made of."

The lights in the room come up. We're standing in a city street at night time. I turn to my team.

"Let's do this," I say. I creep forward, my boot stepping onto the cobbled city street. Suddenly, I can feel the cold evening wind on my cheeks. I shiver. The simulations are always so real. Or what I imagine to be real. I've not left the Institute in a long time. I don't know what the world out there looks like now. All we can see from inside our training building is the city skyscrapers that lie outside of the walls here. We're told that most of them are derelict.

But in this city street, lights illuminate the windows, and the low murmur of chatter comes from inside. The buildings are filled with Inferiors. But they're not our target right now. We need to scout the area and find the rebels on the streets.

"Pair up," I say, "Have each other's back. Zach, with me. Then Elliott and Ronan, Marcia and Minnie. Follow me."

From experience in Combat Training, I know it's always best to head north. That's where the action always is. Not very realistic, but it's still the case. So I creep forwards, keeping to the shadows that the buildings cast. Zach sticks close to my side, obedient, but Elliott strolls through the center of the street in defiance. He even throws in a whistle for good measure, sideways glancing at me and hoping for a reaction. It earns him a giggle from Minnie, even after everything that's happened.

"Get in line, Elliott," I tell him. He ignores me. I sigh, pausing to look at my wristwatch. New settings have been activated for me now, since I'm Team Leader. It takes me a moment to work out the control panel, but then I find the punishment setting. I select Elliott's name on the list and he gasps as a shock of electricity pulses through his wristwatch.

"You didn't just do that," he growls through gritted teeth.

"Get back in line or I'll up the voltage," I hiss. Zach and Ronan exchange a look and I glare at them both. I can feel their disdain, but how else am I meant to get them to listen to me if they refuse to have respect for my position?

"Mind on the task, everyone. Come on."

Everyone obeys this time. I resent that I have to use violence to get their attention. It's something I need to work on, for sure. I know Captain Strauss will be watching, wondering whether she made the right decision when she selected me as Team Leader. I want to close my eyes and give in to the feeling of hopelessness that has rested inside me for some time now. It's exhausting. But I'm not giving up yet. I have a point to prove.

We creep to the end of the block. As we do, I can hear rioting in the streets. Of course, not really, but when you're in the simulation, it feels real. The adrenaline in your veins is real. So are the survival instincts inside you. So I have to ask myself, fight or flight? Fighting now could strengthen the team morale, but it's also dangerous. Maybe not literally, but it could cost us the task. Winning these things is usually about good timing. In this case, maybe waiting for the riots to split up and taking the enemies down in smaller groups is a better call.

"Listen up everyone. We're going to stay together and wait this out a while. I want to see what the Inferiors do."

"Are you kidding? They're in a tight group right there! Toss a grenade in, we'll be finished in seconds," Elliott hisses. I shake my head, running all of our lessons with Captain Strauss through my mind.

"It would also destroy part of the buildings. Buildings that will belong to us once the war is over. Grenades are a last resort," I reason. Zach is clearly not listening to me. His glare is focussed on Elliott.

"You just have to say your piece, don't you, Elliott? Even though your idea is crap, and you know it."

"Fuck off, Zach. I mean it."

"You going to make me, huh? You've got no power over us anymore, Elliott. You're nothing."

I look up and groan. Their fighting has caught the attention of the group of Inferiors. One of them alerts the others and I get my gun out, ready to shoot.

"You two idiots can gun at the front. At least you'll be the first to get hit now. Move it. I'm seriously unimpressed."

When neither of them move, I jab my gun into Elliott's back. "I swear if you don't move, I'll shoot you myself."

The pair of them exchange a glance before heading forwards to shoot. I turn to the girls and Ronan.

"I'm glad to see some of you have some sense. We can't abandon these two, as much as I'd like to, but I want you all to follow me. We're still going to catch them by surprise if we slip through the alleys and fire from behind. Are you with me?"

Marcia and Ronan nod solemnly. Minnie smirks, and at first I think she's going to defy me. Then she grabs her gun from her holster and reloads it.

"You're the boss."

I move off and the others fall in line. Elliott glances behind him to see what we're doing.

"Where the hell are you going?" he asks.

"Stay in position! That's an order."

Elliott scowls, not paying attention to the fight at hand. He'll do anything now to undermine me, I just know it. I watch as one of the Inferiors pulls a gun out and aims perfectly, robotically, at Elliott. A bullet hits his leg and he goes down in agony, the simulation working overtime to make it feel real. There's no time to change the plan now. I have to trust that Zach will handle it. The rest of us head through the alley to strike from the new position. We can see the group annihilating Elliott and Zach.

"No time to waste. Let's take them down. Fire!"

Bullets fly. It's satisfying watching the enemy soldiers fall to their knees, jittering as bullets hit them in the back, the legs, the head. But it's harrowing, too. They look like us. They sound like us when they scream. But they're not like us. They're not even Inferiors. They're worse – fake Inferiors. You don't get much lower than that.

But for once, we're not exactly winning. We will complete the challenge, but our scores will be abysmal. This wasn't a hard task, particularly. Sure, it required a team effort, and it relied on everyone doing their part. But when I see that Elliott, Zach and Marcia have fallen in the fighting, I know how badly this has gone.

Even as I shoot the last Inferior down and we complete the challenge, I know I have failed.

The simulation comes to an end. The scenery fades away to reveal the gray building blocks that make up the arena. The walls peel back to their original positions, resetting the arena for the next team. The tannoy system crackles on to allow Captain Strauss to give her feedback.

"Please stand by for your scores. Remember, as usual, you are looking to score the lowest amount of points possible out of eighty. Your average score is below fifteen, but I should warn you, this time will be an exception."

My heart does a somersault. Am I going to be the reason Team Nine falls from grace? This isn't a good start for me. But I find that no one is looking at me. The rest of the team is tearing one another apart with dirty looks. Most are aimed in Elliott's direction. However, as Captain Strauss clears her throat, everyone stands to immediate attention.

"Building damage score: three. Had Elliott thrown a grenade, the damage would have been far worse. Damage was sustained through Marcia's stray bullets."

The whole team groans. Trust Marcia to make such a dumb mistake. She shrinks back into herself. She knows she's the team liability, though it's not like any of us are on top form today. As team leader, I know I should comfort her or give her some tips, but I'm too agitated and nervous to bother.

"Inferior takedown score: two. A duo escaped via the alleyways that weren't blocked. This would have been easily avoidable had you all followed the original plan. Your efficiency was reasonable, but not to your highest standard."

I can feel anger bubbling inside me. *Imagine how well we could have done if you'd all just listened for once* I think to myself. Of course, I refrain from saying anything out loud. It would be unprofessional to say the least. At least for now, the scores are relatively low. We don't usually score much above twenty, but with the team member scores impending, I have a feeling this is about to get a whole lot worse.

"Team member scores…Marcia scored the highest with eight. Sustained an injury, damaged property and failed to work as a team."

Elliott shoots her a look, but the others are all more patient. They want to know how they did. Or rather, how badly they did. Besides, they're fully aware that none of them are innocent in this scenario.

"Zach, you also scored highly with seven points. A very disappointing performance. Elliott, your score is equal to Zach's. Karissa, I suggest some sort of punishment for poor behavior. This is the only tip I'll give you as a new Team Leader."

I nod solemnly, trying to ignore the gaze of my team members. I can tell they're not happy. I should have had better control, but when personalities like Elliott step forwards, who is ever able to tame them?

"Minerva and Ronan, for keeping to the plan, you scored lower than the others. However, hesitance when faced with orders scores you each three points."

Neither of them respond except with a nod of acceptance. Ronan in particular listens when he is given feedback, and Minnie always knows where she's gone wrong. It doesn't stop her from causing trouble, though.

"And the Team Leader score…"

I hold my breath. This is the moment I've been waiting for. I need her to tell me it's not my fault. I need her to lay the blame on disobedient members of the team. But before she even reveals my score, I know it won't be good.

"Seven points, Karissa. The task was messy and your team didn't listen to you. Since it was your first task, I'll be giving you some time to regroup and I'm sure you can pull it together. However, I expect better. Much better."

I do the maths quickly. Forty points. A clean half score. Forty points is unheard of, especially in Team Nine. Team

Nine who always excel, going above and beyond even when faced with the hardest challenges. Team Nine who have never once crumbled under pressure. Team Nine who have been felled by one simple change.

The result of the challenge couldn't be much worse. As Captain Strauss signs out, I prepare to address my team, but I watch as they ignore my gaping mouth and exit the simulation center in silence, leaving me alone.

RILEY

It's been a long time since I went to a gambling hall, but I'll never forget the smell. The sourness of home-brewed whiskey in the air, the dark mustiness of the underground casino both familiar and unwelcome. Each step I take right now hurts like hell as I recover from my injuries, and I wince as my shoes squelch on the sticky floor. Elianna looks around her in horror, Squid with a grin on his face. Some of us are in our element here. Others aren't.

This is the place where magic happens. Where if I'm clever, I'll double our money and walk away with money jangling in my pockets. I once ruled this place with an iron fist. I can do it again.

I started out in this place when I was nine. It's just ten miles out from the Pits, and it's the town that brought me up until Elianna and I decided to try our luck at the Pits. It took us a few days to get here, given the state I'm in, but now that we're here, I know the difficult trip was worth it.

Back in the day, I bargained my way in as a waitress because my father used to earn his keep behind the bar as a young man. But as I served desperate men with drinks and food, I learned how this place works. I learned every card game in the book, learned how the slot machines are trained to rinse you for everything you've got, learned which games have the best odds with the best payout. I watched men with white gloves on their hands shuffling cards like goddamn magicians, tossing the players their fate as they received each card. And now, I'm returning here with one goal in mind - to play some games.

"Welcome to paradise," I tell my friends with a grin on my face. Elianna wraps her arms around herself. She couldn't look more out of place here if she tried.

"Is this place safe?"

"Is anywhere really safe?" Squid asks, raising his eyebrow. He looks around him with keen curiosity, rubbing his hands together. "So what's the plan here? We're making money, right?"

I grin. "That's right. If we play this right, we'll be walking away with enough money to get us all the X drug. And then we'll be laughing."

"Do you…do you think this will work?" Tiger asks, his forehead creased. "I mean…isn't everyone here to do the same? And…and aren't gambling halls designed to take your money?"

I wave him off. "Relax. I know what I'm doing. This place raised me. Let's get ourselves some drinks, relax a little. By the end of the night, I promise we'll be rolling in cash."

"You can't possibly be talking about getting drunk, Riley. It's one thing to be gambling sober, but drunk? Besides, you're only fourteen. You're too young to drink," Elianna chastised.

"Too young to drink but not too young to fight to the death in the Pits for entertainment?" I snap back. Given that Elianna is the one who shut me out in the first place, I'm not feeling in the mood for her sudden maternal advice. "Get over yourself. I'm ordering a whiskey and so are you. They won't be turning away paying customers today."

I'm right about that, at least. As I order at the bar, shouting over the loud music, the bartender eyes me up suspiciously, but makes my drinks anyway. Squid whoops as he takes up his drink. At least someone is grateful to be here. Tiger and Elianna hold their drinks close to their chests, looking at them as though they're poisoned. I sigh. They're hardly going to fit in here, but that's not my problem. I'm the breadwinner here. I need to look confident, and it's easier to do that when you've drained to the bottom of your glass. I sip the bitter drink and make my way through the crowds.

The place is a cacophony of noise. The rumble of coins falling from slot machines, cheers from roulette tables when someone wins a round, tense murmurings as the banker and player face off in baccarat. Even the silence at the poker tables is loud, groups of people gathered around holding their breaths to see who will fold and who will take a chance.

I know that casinos have been around for years, that the odds have never truly been fair, but as I walk through, I can see that the mood is tenser than it used to be. Now that money is the difference between life and death, between X drug or no X drug, the stakes are at an all time high. No one is betting with small money anymore. Each game will end with someone's downfall, a fall from grace that no one will come back from. It's more ruthless than the last time I was here, but so is the rest of the world. What do we have to lose by trying? Sure, the money we have could save one of us. But I don't want this unless we're all walking away with a chance to live. And, hey. At least if we lose here, we'll have fun doing it.

There's a tremor of excitement inside me. I feel guilty for wanting this, for feeling a pull toward this place, but it's been years since I last let go. I take another sip of my whiskey as though it doesn't burn my throat. Haven't we earned the chance to indulge a little? After everything we've been through? Walking through this place, I understand how it must feel to be part of the elite. To know that even though the world is crashing and burning outside, there's still something for us here. A chance to live life on the edge, to be messy, to make expensive mistakes with something to fall back on.

If only we had that luxury.

Whatever I do here, I'm going to have to be clever about it. It's about patience as much as anything. Waiting for slot machines to free up that haven't won in a while. Watching the way other poker players move before joining the table. Calculating risk versus reward. I guess my friends don't trust me to be able to make those kinds of decisions. They think I'm reckless, born to fight, not to think. But I'll prove them wrong when we walk out of here with so much money we can't fit it all in our pockets.

I weave through the place, the others trailing behind me like a bad smell. Squid seems enthused by this whole place, at least. He's too bloody stupid to be of much use to me here, although I could maybe stick him on the slots and hope for the best. Elianna and Tiger are the ones with brains inside their heads, not him. But he'll be good company while I'm raking in the dosh. Tonight isn't about that though. Tonight is for getting the lay of the land, having a few drinks, letting loose for a while. I'll start placing bets tomorrow.

And I'll win.

As I'm walking around, I catch sight of someone who holds my attention a little longer than the desperate punters. She's standing on the balcony that overlooks the entire casino. I've never been up there, but I know that the balcony is reserved for the players who are playing to a higher level. It's a place where anything goes - russian roulette, all or nothing kind of rounds, people betting things beyond money. If she's up there, she's either an expert player, or she's the one running this entire show.

The woman is beautiful, there's no denying that. I've never had an interest in love or the like, but I can still recognize beauty when I see it. It helps that she also looks expensive in her red coat with a glass of champagne clutched in her manicured hands. My hand runs over my shorn hair as I admire her box braids, wondering how much she was able to pay someone to do her hair for her.

She's the kind of woman I aspire to be. In a position of

power, not letting anyone mess her around, running the show with a glass in hand and no cares in the world. I watch long enough that I catch her attention and she looks down on me in what seems like amusement. I don't break eye contact. I'm not scared to show my face here. She should get familiar with it. I'm going to be here a lot.

"What's first?" Squid asks, tapping my shoulder like an excitable kid. I forget sometimes that he's not that much older than me. I wonder if he's ever been to a place like this, enjoyed a night like this. There's an eager look on his face that makes my heart hurt. I raise my glass to him with a smile.

"I say we get a bit pissed and just enjoy ourselves. What do you think?"

Squid grins. "I think you have the best ideas, kid. I'm in."

Tiger and Elianna are still skulking close by. I raise an eyebrow at them both.

"What do you say? You up for it?"

Tiger hesitates and then nods. "Alright. Just one night."

I grin and offer him a high five. "That's what I'm talking about. Looks like you're outnumbered, Elianna."

"I might have said yes," Elianna says indignantly. "I'm not completely dull, Riley."

I snort. "Yeah? Prove it."

Elianna wavers before knocking back the entire glass of whiskey in her hand. I laugh in surprise as she winces, but she doesn't complain. I throw an arm around her waist and after a moment, her arm wraps around my shoulder. It feels almost as warm as the whiskey in my stomach. I lean into her. I can put our quarrels aside for a moment. Maybe for tonight, we can just forget that there's anything bad in our lives. Perhaps we can spend this night learning how to laugh again. I push thoughts of our fallen friends aside. Our ghosts can haunt us in the morning.

Just tonight, I want to try out being normal.

RAVEN

I knew the costumes we wore for the mission would be ridiculous, but I'm not sure any of us were really expecting what Logan brings us for the mission. I stare blankly at him as he hands me a pair of gold leather trousers and a top that is cropped at the stomach and made entirely of feathers. I pull at the pants gingerly. There's almost no give in the material. They're going to suffocate my legs.

"Seriously? This is what we are expected to wear?"

Logan grins at me, flicking a feather on the strange garment. "It was practically made for you. You are a Raven, after all."

I shake my head at him, examining the clothes carefully. "I can't believe people wear this on a regular basis…"

It's close to what my mother used to wear when she worked for Logan's father. That thought makes me feel a little sick. I don't want any connection back to that dark part of our lives. But now, I have a mission to complete. I can't be distracted. Everyone at the school is relying on me and the others and I need to focus on the people left alive, not the ones who are dead.

Logan seems to be thinking along the same lines. He has a determined look on his face as he oversees everyone's costume choices. While Ellis and June struggle into their outfits, he tugs off his grubby white shirt and collects a blue silk one from the pile of items he's gathered. He ties the bottom of it in an expert bow so that his stomach is exposed. I've seen him in clothes like this before, so it doesn't feel completely strange to me. After all, as much as he tries to hide it, Logan isn't one of us. He's fancy folk - he's the reason we know anything about uptown fashion at all, but it still sets him apart from us. He's doing his best, but no one is ever going to accept him the same. Except me, of course.

I feel the same way about Valeria. With her dyed hair and healthy body, you can tell she doesn't belong among us. In fact, I'm not entirely sure why she's here with us. While Logan is young and rebellious, here to support me more than anything, she has less incentive to screw the system, as far as I know. Maybe, for whatever reason, she's not eligible for the X Drug.

"Are we leaving soon?" she asks, appearing in a short top that shows off the muscles of her stomach. I'm beginning to see a trend in the style of clothing. It's totally impractical and I can't help thinking how hard it's going to be to run in these pants, but we have to blend in or we're never going to make it within a mile of the supermarket. I think of my grubby outfit that I've been wearing for weeks on end. They'd take one look at me and have me shot.

"As soon as everyone's ready, we'll go. We have to look the part," I say. Roger appears in an ill-fitting shirt of his own, grimacing.

"The sooner we can get out of these outfits, the better," he says, rolling his eyes at the flared sleeves he's sporting. "My boyfriend would have a field day if he saw me wearing this."

"This isn't a time to be complaining about clothing," Ellis says bitterly, though she herself keeps fiddling with the waistband of her trousers. She turns to me. "Come on. We haven't got all day."

I try not to let my irritation show, but Ellis really is a piece of work. I know we have our differences, but doesn't she realize that we're on the same side here? I ignore her comment and call the team together. They band up in front of me, a group of obvious misfits. I clear my throat.

"Here's the plan. When we arrive at the supermarket, Logan, June and I will head inside for supplies. Meanwhile, Roger, Valeria, and Ellis can go around the back to investigate the stock room and the delivery van. We will then need to dispose of any workers who could give us away. That means anyone in the stock room and anyone who is on delivery duty. Once the van is secure, the rest of us are going to need to get the supplies out to the back. Logan has been here before, and he says there's a back door available to get into the alleyway. Valeria will be prepared to drive away, and she will also have her weapon in case things go badly. Any questions?"

"What if things go wrong?" June says timidly. "I think your plan is good...better than what we came up with. But...there could be a lot of room for error. What if someone is caught or hurt?"

I don't really know how to respond to that question. I know the answer is a simple one - we have to fight for ourselves. Leave the injured behind. It's survival of the fittest. It's something Valeria and Logan might not understand, but for the rest of us, the ones among us who have spent our lives fighting for food, for a roof over our heads, for each breath we take, it makes complete sense. I fix June a meaningful look. She swallows hard and nods, understanding my meaning entirely. Logan is the only one who seems confused, but I don't feel like explaining to him that this mission might risk his life.

"Let's get going," I say. For a moment, I feel like no one is listening. Then, one by one my team step up to my side. As a unit, we make our way to the supermarket.

The walk through the streets is nerve-wracking. This is the riskiest mission we have attempted so far. Usually, our food runs consist of a small unit running through abandoned buildings for scraps. Now, we're walking into a situation where we have no idea what the result might be. We stick out like sore thumbs, too. In the war-ravaged streets, we look more than a little suspicious in our ridiculous outfits. If we come across any rebels now, we could be in serious danger. We're designed to look as though we are part of the elite - the ones who are going to come out from all of this even better off than they were before. We're walking targets, and Valeria, in particular, seems to be aware of this. She walks in her quiet, cold manner with her hand gripped around the gun in her overcoat pocket. She's barely said a word to any of us. June is walking with Ellis, making nervous chatter while Ellis responds with silence. Logan walks ahead, leading us to the supermarket. I also get the sense that he feels protective of the group. He keeps glancing back at me and offering me a hesitant smile. I nod to him each time to let him know that I'm okay. I'm keeping my cards close to my chest. Of course I'm scared, but I can't let it show. That's not my job here. Especially with Ellis glaring at me every now and then, I can't afford to be weak.

As we get a little closer to our destination, Roger falls in step with me. I hate to admit it, but having him close makes me feel a little safer. Like Valeria, he has this air about him, like he always knows exactly what he's doing. There's no uncertainty in his gait, and he doesn't seem nervous at all. He's got a knife in his pocket and every now and then, he takes it out and plays with it, his nimble fingers wielding it with ease.

But the more I look at him, the less I trust his charming exterior. I know his sort. He's got a tattoo on his wrist - a simple set of three dots - that represent one of the local gangs. He doesn't try and hide it, but Valeria has been eyeing it up ever since I formed the team. They're from different worlds, though Roger is so sleek that he almost looks like he belongs in the upper echelons. He doesn't look like someone who has been fighting for his life on the streets.

Still, his gang status doesn't surprise me. Young men and women often get roped in, especially the ones who are physically able. They get more access to food and weapons, and that can be life-changing if you've lost your parents, your home, your livelihood. Several gangs have tried to recruit me in the past, but it's not for me. It would mean leaving Jonah behind, for one thing. I don't blame people for getting involved, but it's even more dangerous than stealing from the markets. High stakes, high rewards, I guess. Roger certainly doesn't seem like he struggles the same way as I do, as June does, or Ellis. I guess even within the downtown society, there are tiers of status.

"I've seen you around," Roger comments. He chooses this moment to take out his knife and play with it. I know for a fact that the move is deliberate, like he wants me to know how handy he is with that thing. Suddenly, I don't feel so safe around him.

"I doubt that," I tell him bluntly. We may be on a team, but I don't plan to engage much in this conversation. If Roger is in a gang, he's got dangerous connections. I want to remain on neutral ground with him. He clicks his tongue in thought.

"No, I definitely have. You've got a face I wouldn't forget. Perhaps I've seen you at the markets? My leader has always been fond of the kids from around the markets. Says you're the quickest and smartest."

"Well, my family wouldn't have survived so long otherwise."

"Exactly. So there's no way we've not been in contact before," he insists, looking me up and down. Logan turns around once again to check on me and I grit my teeth. He's making me look pitiful with every move he makes. There's no way Roger hasn't picked up on it. He smirks at me, raising an eyebrow.

"He checks up on you an awful lot."

"He's checking on the team."

"Nah. He's looking at you. Anyone with eyes can see that," he says. After a moment, he puts his knife back in his pocket. Perhaps he doesn't feel threatened by my presence anymore. "So Logan and you are friends, right? He says you guys go way back."

He's making it sound like casual conversation, but I know how it works with guys like him. They use everything against you. They collect little tidbits of information until they have enough information to crush you. Secrets of any kind are currency, and though my feelings for Logan aren't entirely a secret, they're a weakness. I can see him noting this exchange. *Raven's weak spot: Logan Golding.* I curse Logan for being so open and trusting. He has no idea how to deal with guys like Roger. I make a mental note never to mention that I have a brother around Roger.

"We were friends once, yes. I haven't seen him for years," I say honestly. Roger looks smug.

"Well, he certainly seems to be fond of you. I guess it's nice, having someone to watch your back like that…"

I'm beginning to trust this guy less and less by the minute. He's only a few years older than me by the looks of things, but he's clearly a lot smarter than I anticipated. I'll bet he's high up in the gang he works for. Damn Logan for telling me to bring him. He's here for himself, but also for his gang - that's clear now. I need to tread lightly, but I also need something to use against him, should our uneasy alliance break down any time soon. I kick a large stone across the cobbles as we continue walking, keeping my eyes on the ground.

"You've got someone watching your back too. Your boyfriend, right?"

Roger seems to have been expecting this question. He doesn't miss a beat. "Yeah, that's Drew. Though to be honest, he couldn't watch my back if he tried. He's not tough the way I am. He's going to have to learn to fight for himself before he can do anything for me."

"Doesn't sound like you have much faith in him."

I see irritation cross Roger's face and I have to hide a smile. Logan looks back at me once again and smiles, tilting his head to encourage me to join him.

"You should go," Roger says with a tinge of bitterness in his voice. "Then he can stop checking on you every two seconds."

I'd do almost anything to get away from Roger right now. I can tell the two of us aren't going to be friends. Everyone else might think he's a nice guy, but I see through him, and he hasn't even bothered to try with me. If he knows me from the markets, maybe he senses I'm much too streetwise to fall for his little act.

I fall into step with Logan and he threads his arm through mine. I know it's an uptown custom so I let him do it, even though his arm against mine feels so strange. It's been a long time since we touched, but I've missed the sensation, as much as I don't want to admit that to myself. He clears his throat.

"Getting acquainted with Roger?"

I shrug. I don't want to tell him my concerns about him until I'm ready. "I guess so. Why'd you call me over? You missing me or something?"

A playful smile appears on his lips. "Maybe. Although I've spent a long time missing you, Raven. I bet I could've survived a few more minutes. I just like your company."

I feel my cheeks flushing. Logan has always been a distraction to me. A distraction from what's important. I always knew, even when we were young, that the way he made my stomach flit and my heart soar meant a lot more than friendship. I never got to find out if he felt the same. His constant flirting made it hard to tell if he really felt something for me at all, but there really wasn't time to figure that out, as much as I wanted to. There's never been a good time.

"I'm good company to keep. I've got your back," I tell him. "Look...if something happens to me today...you'll take care of Jonah, right?"

"You think it's more likely I'll make it out alive than you?" Logan snorts. "Raven...you've got this. The way you stepped up earlier...you're in your element. Don't doubt yourself."

Here I am, blushing again. He really does know exactly how to get me, even after four years apart. I shake my head to myself, hoping to forget the comment. The scenery around us is changing, anyway. I'm beginning to get the sense we were somewhere posh. The streets are widening out as though paving the way for success and prosperity. It's a far cry from the cramped conditions back in the inner city. There are some cars here too, and somehow, there's less smog here, as though the air is filtered for the rich folk's enjoyment.

There are blocks of flats, but they don't tower right toward the clouds, and I can see atop the roof that there are gardens nestled among the solar panels. It seems like the people who need those gardens the least to grow food get access to them while the rest of us starve.

"You okay?" Logan asks me. I sigh.

"Yeah. Just taking it all in."

As we walk, Valeria veers to the pavement and gives me a nod. I nod back. She's going to find the van we can use to take the deliveries back to the school. We're going to join her soon to carry out the plan.

This is it.

I try to push away my nerves as we approach the supermarket. I feel like I don't fit in here, even in my fancy clothes. I think I'd be better suited to going with Valeria, Roger and Ellis. I know how to use my fists, at least. But this is new terrain. I have to blend in and it's scaring me more than anything else that might happen here.

Logan reaches into his pocket and finds the three valid ration cards that we have. June is taking Valeria's and I'm taking Lark's, hoping that his name will pass as a girl's. There are no pictures or personal information aside from names on the ration cards, but I've memorized the code on it to ensure it works for me.

The plan is simple, in theory. We pretend to be normal shoppers as we walk around the supermarket. With our ration cards in hand, nothing about us will seem suspicious. June will pile as much as she can in her cart and then run for the van, making a noisy exit from the building to alert security. While the cashiers chase her down, we'll make a run for it with our own groceries out of the back entrance and make it to the van where Valeria will be waiting to drive us away. If anything goes wrong, she will pull out her gun to ward off the security.

What could go wrong?

Plenty. Because when we arrive, the supermarket is heaving with people. I try not to look concerned as I join the gaggle of people waiting outside. I peer over them and see that there's a security guard blocking them off at the door.

"You'll have to wait your turn," the guard insists to the crowd.

"I don't like to be kept waiting," a man says with pursed lips. "What's the hold up?"

"We're only allowing a few in at a time. We've had to up the security measures, there are a lot of thieves around at the moment. Plus, people are trying to take more than their share. There is no need for panic buying. You're all safe, and we're not going to run out of stock."

Must be nice, I think, *knowing your privilege will shelter you while everyone else is running amok.*

I glance at Logan, knowing our plan is going to leave us exposed. This isn't going to be easy now. The plan is full of holes. I feel fear rising inside me, but there's no time to change things up. We'll look suspicious if we start whispering among ourselves. We have to stick with what we decided.

We queue for a while to be let inside. As we get to the front, the three of us cluster together. However, as we all try to enter with the next wave, the guard puts his hand up to June.

"We're over capacity. You'll have to wait."

"We always shop together!" Logan says indignantly, perfectly tapping into his uptown privileged persona. "Let us pass…"

"I'm sorry, sir, but the rules apply to everyone. Take it or leave it."

My heart is beating fast as we silently leave June behind. We're a man down. Most importantly, she's the one who is supposed to make the run. I could do it myself, but it's a risk without communicating the plan to the others. I should've let her in first, but the security guard has already ushered us inside, leaving June alone outside.

This is hopeless. We can't hang around waiting for her or we'll look suspicious. But we have to try. We've come this far and people are counting on us. I feel for the knife in my pocket and find some comfort in knowing I can use it if I need to. Logan puts his hand on the small of my back for a moment to soothe me and I feel better. *Deep breath,* I think, *it's time to do this.*

The supermarket is a maze to me. It's so bright in here with its white walls and lights hanging over every aisle. The shelves are stocked with brightly packaged things that I've never seen before. It's hard to believe that people come here all of the time and shop for these things weekly while the rest of us beg for scraps at the markets.

But according to Lark's ration card, he's allowed much more than I am when I do my weekly shop. His parents are doctors, and doctors are given extra rations for their service. I can't argue with that, and yet as I absentmindedly pick up items from the shelves, following Logan's lead, I feel deprived. Could this life have been mine if my mother had agreed to marry Logan's father? If I'd been born rich, would my heart be racing right now as I do something as mundane as walking around a supermarket?

"Darling, don't forget to pick up rice," Logan calls over his shoulder with a wink. He's enjoying himself far too much.

But June, who has finally made it inside, looks completely uncomfortable. It's clear, like me, she's never seen such splendor on offer all at once. I turn my head away from her and look for rice. I find it in a blue cardboard box and check the price, holding my breath. It's more expensive than anything I've ever bought at the market. It can't be worth what these people pay for it, and yet there's no way anyone in this shop goes without the staples.

Maybe the system isn't so perfect after all.

I continue through the store, placing things in my trolley. I try to imagine that this feels normal to me, grabbing whatever I feel like in the moment, but I can't. I'll never know the ease of this kind of life, especially now. If I'd run away with Logan then maybe I would've made this my reality. But how could I stomach it while the rest of the world is starving? Now that I've known both sides of the coin, I know I'll always choose the one I was born into, even if it means that I die penniless.

I take my cart up to the tills where Logan is already queuing up. June is a little flustered as she meanders her cart toward the till beside us, and her eyes are on the exit. I can sense her nerves a mile off, but if she can pull this off, no one will go hungry tonight. It has to be worth a shot.

Logan chats cheerily to the cashier and I wait, my hands gripped around the trolley tight. I can feel my heartbeat in my ears. My palms are sweating.

And then June runs for it.

June's trolley crashes past the cashier and through the front door before anyone clocks what's going on. The security guard is busy controlling the crowd of uptowners outside and is slow to respond. As he begins to chase June down the street, we make our move. I swing the trolley around, almost knocking a man behind me over, and I run for the back exit of the store.

A rush of exhilaration takes over me as I run for the door with Logan just ahead of me. The cashier shouts out indignantly, calling for more security, but they're occupied with June already. Our trolleys collide with various objects, but we're moving fast. We make it to the back door and Logan opens the door for me, allowing me through. I stumble clumsily into the open air, my chest tight. There's a narrow alley and I can see the delivery vans up ahead. That's where Valeria will be.

We make a run for it, Logan taking the lead. He laughs to himself, more out of nerves than anything, I think. My legs ache as my feet pound the pavement. We're going to make it. We're going to make-

Something hard slams into my back and I let go of the trolley, falling to the ground. I cry out and try to scramble to my feet, but someone kicks me hard in the stomach. The air leaves me. It brings tears to my eyes as I try to crawl away, but another blow to my stomach leaves me in agony and washed over by nausea.

"Thought you could get away with it?" a man's voice growls. I look up and see a security guard towering over me. He's holding a heavy baton in his hand, and I know now that he's willing to use it on me. "Thought you could cheat us like that? Scum. Not so brave now, are you?"

"I'm just trying to feed my friends," I sob, curling into myself to try and stop the pain in my stomach. "Please, just let me go…"

The man grabs the back of my hair and pulls me to face him. He slams the baton into my thigh and I crumple back to my knees, dizzied by the bruising impact.

"You're not one of us," he snarls. "This is exactly what we're trying to eliminate from our society. You-"

A gunshot explodes around my ears. The man jumps but doesn't let go of me. I twist around and see that someone has come to help me.

"Let go," Valeria growls. She's holding the pistol right in front of the cashier's face. "Do you want to die?"

He shakes his head. "No...please just let me go…"

"Give me the baton."

He does as she asks, letting go of my hair as he does. My scalp feels raw from where he yanked at my hair and my body feels badly bruised.

"Let go of her before I blow your face off," Valeria says so calmly that it sends a shiver down my spine. The man lets me go without hesitation. Valeria nods at him again, her eyes icy cold.

"Step back. Good man."

He does. He keeps retreating until he's a few meters away. Valeria grabs my arm and pushes me behind her, telling me to run for the van.

Valeria helps me to my feet without a word, pushing me in the direction of the van. I'm completely rattled, but instinct takes over and I begin to run, grabbing the handles of the trolley once again and pushing it toward the van. Through the pain, through my desperation to collapse, I make my escape. Because this has to be worth it. After the terror I just endured, this thing has to be worth it.

Roger and Ellis are waiting in the back of the van and they help me load up the trolley into the vehicle. I feel dizzy as I stumble in after them, shutting the doors behind me. Logan is sitting in the front of the van, waiting for Valeria to return. We might've got away with this.

"Raven? Are you alright?" Logan asks. "What took you?"

"Just a little hold up," I groan, slumping against the side of the van. I've taken a few hits in my life, but the sting of the baton on my back is like nothing I've ever experienced. Now that the adrenaline is leaving my body it hurts even worse.

Valeria and June come hurtling into the van, breathless as Valeria puts the key in the ignition. I can't help but wonder how she got the guts to come and help me. She could've just left me behind. I'm expendable. But as she does a quick headcount, I can see that she cares. Beneath her quiet, stony exterior, she's good through and through.

"Hold tight," she says, revving up the engine. "Let's try and get back in one piece…"

RILEY

My stomach is churning like a damn tornado this morning. I sit up with damp clothes clinging to my skin and cold air hitting my face. My head spins. Looks like I've got my first hangover.

I realize that we slept on the street last night, in a spot along a chain link fence. There are some tents set up around here on patches of dirt that are long abandoned, but mostly, people just sleep out in the open, left to the elements. Now *this* takes me back to the days before the Pits. The days after I lost my parents and I had nowhere else to go. The cold tarmac beneath me is like an old friend. An old friend that constantly lets me down, more like.

But I feel good in some ways. I close my eyes and remember how last night, I couldn't stop laughing. I remember how my head spun as fast as the roulette wheel, how Squid and I spent the whole night clutching one another and making crude jokes and watching other people losing their money. There wasn't a happier pair in the entire place.

Even Elianna and Tiger let go a little. The pair of them sat to one side most of the time, but even they shared a few smiles once the drinks kicked in. For a while, all the bad thoughts got pushed aside, taking up residence somewhere out of sight and out of mind.

But there's this feeling deeper inside me that makes me feel a little uncomfortable. I wrap my arms around my knees, feeling a cold shudder running down my back. My mood feels bottomless, like there's a deeper level I can sink to. I feel the squeeze of anxiety in my twisted stomach. I guess everything is catching up to me now. Putting off a problem doesn't make it go away.

It was nice not to dream last night, because whenever I do, I'm taken back to the Pits. For so long, I lived life there as though it didn't affect me. All those lives I ended blur into one. But with Bull it was different. It was personal. And I'll never be able to shake off how much it hurt me to hurt her. I wish I could turn back time. I wish that I could have just let her win. The problem is I've never really been very good at losing. And I had so much I didn't want to leave behind.

Was it worth it, though? A night of happiness in a casino? Is that worth everything I did to her?

A silent sob ripples through my chest. I'm no damn crier, but today's got me in my feelings. I hug my knees closer to my body and rest my throbbing forehead against them, sinking into the deep hole I've dug for myself. I tell myself it's just the hangover. I can climb out of this. But right in this moment, it feels like nothing will ever be right again.

"Riley?"

I snap my head up. Next to me, Elianna has woken up and is staring at me. The last thing I need is for her to see me cry.

"Hmm?" I say, wiping my eyes quickly. Elianna searches my face, her eyes softening in concern.

"Are you alright? You don't look so great."

I jut my chin up. "Of course I am. I'm just a little woozy. You would be too if you'd let your hair down a bit more."

Elianna hangs her head. "How long are you going to be like this with me, Riley? I'm sorry about what I said to you, back at the Pits. I know that's what is on your mind."

I clench my fists. Those words she said to me haunt me

everyday. *Sometimes I think you don't have a damn heart.* It's like she doesn't know me at all. Like she doesn't see that behind my stupid grins and stupid jokes, I'm so, so small, curled up inside myself to hold my feelings close to me. Behind all my loud banter and wild nature, my biggest fears loom inside me and try to eat me alive. Fears of being alone, of getting too attached, of losing what I have left in this world. And I'm not talking about money. There are things that go way beyond that.

"You haven't said you're sorry. Not properly," I mutter. Elianna shuffles closer and wraps her arms around me. I don't want to give in to her, to let her know she's won, but tears prick my eyes again and I know that she has.

"I *am* sorry. I really am. I know what you did for us. I know that none of us would've survived without what happened. I just…sometimes I have trouble coming to terms with it. How we live."

I nod. We all know this isn't how it's meant to be. In another life, we would still have parents around to take care of us, but instead we fight every day to stay alive. None of us are expected to live to be adults. But we're still here, against the odds. It's only that fact that lifts my heart a little from how low it has sunk. Knowing that it could still be worse than lying out on the cold street with a hangover and our lives hanging in the balance. We could be dead. We could be starving. But we'll make it through today. We're survivors and that's what we do.

I sniff quietly, hoping Elianna has miraculously not noticed how upset I am. "Yeah, well. I had to make a choice. And when I really think about it…I'd do it again. But only for you. For Squid. For Tiger. I did it for you guys."

"I know you did," Elianna whispers, propping her chin on my head. I wince. It's still not fully healed from the fight in the Pits. But I don't want her to move. For a while I want someone to hold me like this. I might not crave romantic love the way most do, but this is what I live for. Knowing someone loves me, even when I'm a nightmare and I feel like a burden on the world. Knowing someone will still care even when I'm the biggest mess in the world. Elianna may criticize me and my choices, but I know that no one in the world loves me as much as she does. No one has put up with me for as long as she has. It makes me turn to cling to her a little harder.

I guess for as long as I have her, everything might be okay.

I hear Squid groan and sit up next to Tiger. One side of his face is red and dimpled from having it pressed against the ground. There's a bleary look in his eyes that tells me he's far from well rested.

"Oh man, I keep forgetting how much it sucks to sleep on tarmac," Squid complains. "And my head hurts so bad. Like, so bad you wouldn't believe it."

"You're talking to two girls who were beaten to an inch of their lives this month. I literally have a stab wound in my shoulder. Don't be a damn wimp," I tell him. Elianna laughs quietly and Squid looks at us with narrowed eyes.

"I knew me being your favorite wouldn't last, Riley," he says, but I can tell he's teasing. I sit up straighter and stretch my arms above my head. I have no way to tell the time aside from the sun above our heads. I guess it's close to midday. There are people shuffling on by, getting on with their day. They're not interested in bums like us.

I cast a glance back toward the casino. There are other campers nearby, all of them waiting for it to reopen for the evening, ready to risk it all for some cash to line their pockets. Tonight, when our hangovers have waned, we'll do this thing for real. Now that I've got a lay of the land and figured out the mood there, I can really play the game. I turn to Squid and Elianna.

"Sober up. Tonight, we're hitting the tables."

The casino welcomes us back with open arms. I've mostly recovered from last night's antics and I feel ready to test the waters. I'm not going all in straight away. There's no chance that I'm going on a table where the blinds are almost bigger than the prize pot. Besides, I've been away for a while. I need to ease back into it.

I know just where to go. The casino is a maze that not many people know how to navigate, but I push my way deeper into the room. The front of house is where flashy players go to win, where the crowds draw in to watch the risky plays. The further back we venture, that's where the smaller games take place with less experienced players. I'm guessing there won't be many inexperienced players anymore, though. Why gamble on a game you don't know how to win?

But there will definitely be players that I'm interested in competing with. A few easy games that won't boost my ego too much. It's easy to get cocky when you're on a winning streak, and my ego is big enough these days. I want to steal some easy money and not make myself believe that it has anything to do with skill. I know these players back here can offer me that.

My friends trail behind me. I told them they could go and gamble or drink if they wanted, but Squid seems eager to watch me play, and I know Elianna and Tiger have no interest in this place. So it looks like I've got an audience for tonight. I hope I'm not too rusty.

I opt to start with poker. It's more strategic than some of the other games, which means that if I'm playing with idiots, I can probably win with a pair of twos. I scout out the area. It really is depressing back here. It smells like unwashed bodies and beer because no one can afford anything better. One table in particular makes my lips turn up in a smile. It's the perfect place to start.

I walk up to the table with my chin held high, not wanting to look hesitant as I do. The dealer eyes me up suspiciously.

"No children at the tables," he says to me, dismissing me as he looks away. I slide onto one of the stools anyway.

"It's lucky I'm not a child then," I say, cocking my head to the side. "Children don't win at poker."

The dealer scoffs and rolls his eyes, but doesn't fight it

any further. Everyone knows that these places only pretend to follow the rules. What's the point in turning me away in such a lawless country? I live in an age where kids can do what they want. Drink, smoke, gamble. As long as I'm paying, no one truly bats an eye. I just happen to be one of the few kids around here who actually has the money to try my hand.

Besides, I picked this table for a reason. The round table houses a group of men sagging over the table like they're already resigned to losing their money. Men with scraps of metal punched through their ears, noses, eyebrows, beards, cheeks. They murmur among themselves at my arrival, grumbling of their misfortunes over watered down beer. Two of them clink their pitchers together, a delicate noise in the midst of broken masculine egos and despair.

And one of them is a familiar face to me.

Eros is a regular here. A regular loser. He's been coming here since I was a kid to squander his money. He's terrible at poker and I'll bet he hasn't learned any new tricks over the years. His face is like a map, navigating me to his poorly veiled bluffs every single time. It's like he doesn't even understand the cards in front of him half the time. I used to watch him while I was waiting on the tables. He'd lose his money night after night after night. His friends would laugh about what a fool he was, but he just seemed happy to be there.

And I've got no issue with taking money from a big idiot like that.

I catch his eye as I rest my elbows on the table, waiting to be dealt my cards. A wave of familiarity crosses his face.

"Do I know you?" he asks me, biting at the silver ring in his lip. I shrug.

"I doubt it."

"Huh. Could've sworn I did. You playing a round?"

"No, I'm just sitting here for the fun of it."

Eros laughs as though I've told the best joke in the world. "Alright, missy. I see you've got some attitude. At least you'll keep us entertained while we're losing our money."

The other men at the table grumble. Eros appears to be the only one in a good mood. I assume it's because he's got nothing to lose.

"Trying your luck for the X drug?" Eros asks, glancing at his cards. I watch his eyebrows crease not so subtly. He's got a shit hand.

"I guess."

"Well, good luck to you. My wife told me I should stop coming here now with everything going on, but I've got plenty of money to lose. I always have done."

The comment leaves a bitter feeling inside me. "Perhaps you should go on one of the tables with higher stakes then. Since money is no object."

He laughs again, not seeming to realize that he's pissed me off. "Nah, takes the fun out of the game if you lose it all. Still, you've got some sense starting small. Lives are being ruined in this room tonight."

And I'm here to ruin yours, I think to myself. If I have to stay here all night, I'll empty his pockets completely. That's what I came to do. Play smart, play hard, win it all.

"Take up your cards, girl," the dealer tells me. "And I'm not babying you if you don't know how to play."

"Oh don't worry about me," I say, glancing quickly at my hand before placing it back down on the table. "Worry about this sorry lot. It's their money I'll be taking."

Now I've got their attention. I rest my chin on my hand and wait for the dealer to get the ball rolling. With the blinds paid and the cards dealt, there's no going back now.

I can feel my friends practically breathing down my neck as they watch the game begin. I wish they'd take themselves elsewhere, they're kind of ruining my vibe. I want these men to know that I'm taking them down single handedly. But my friends stay and I focus on the table before me. It's a chancey game, but it's also about presence. It's about intimidating the others at the table. It's about weeding them out mercilessly until you take everything from them. It strikes me as sick that we're doing this. First the government decides to destroy us, and now we're doing it to one another, disguising it as a game. But I have others relying on me, as I always do. I can't afford to be sentimental to people I don't know.

I can't afford to feel sorry for them as I crush them.

The first three cards of five that lie in the middle of the table are overturned. I take them in without picking up my cards again or allowing my face to show anything at all. One man throws down his cards, arms folded and lip pouted. I don't smile, though I want to. This is going to be child's play.

Eros chuckles to himself. He obviously thinks he's got this one in the bag. Judging by what's on the table, it's not hard to guess that he's running for a straight. My stomach clenches a little, knowing there's a possibility that he might have a winning hand, but I play it cool. There are two more cards to play with. It's not over yet.

"Check," the man to my left says. Eros nods, grinning to himself.

"Check. For now."

"And me," I say, wanting the game to move along. There's only four of us still in it, but the next card turning over will discount at least a few of us.

I know I'm right when a four shows up on the table.

"Fold," the man to my left says immediately. I guess he's seen by the twinkle in Eros' eyes that he's about to put down some silly bet. Eros catches my eye. He wants to see what I'm made of.

"What do you say we...raise the stakes?"

It's the response I've been hoping for. He's getting cocky. I can practically look through his cards and see the hand he's got. But it won't stop me from playing along.

I've got him right where I want him.

"Sure."

Eros pushes a pile of chips toward the center of the table. "Raise."

The other player tuts and folds. But I hold fast. I match Eros with ease. Behind me, I hear Elianna's intake of breath.

She thinks I'm being reckless. But I'm the one at the table, not her. I'm sticking with my choice.

"Shall we play the final card?" Eros asks wolfishly.

"Are you the dealer or am I?" the dealer grumbles, but he turns the card over for us all to see. I keep my face straight. I can't let Eros see which way it has swung my luck. Eros drums his fingers on the table. He's giddy with excitement.

"Check," I say. Eros nods quickly.

"Yes, yes, check."

The dealer looks me in the eye and raises his eyebrow. I keep my face level and turn back to the game. Eros is keenly turning over his two cards.

"Straight."

The simultaneous intake of breath around the table didn't surprise me. It could easily be a winning hand. I should be about to lose everything. But I know better. I lay my cards down.

"Straight flush," I say with a grin. The other men are gasping now and the smile has dropped right off Eros' face. It doesn't take long for it to return, though. He laughs out loud as I collect my pile of chips. I've more than doubled what I started with.

"Damn, kid. Must be beginner's luck," Eros says. "Another, dealer! We're just getting started."

That we are, I think to myself. *I'm going to rinse you all.*

KARISSA

I wake with a start from another dream about the white room. It's like I can't escape it. Every time my body shuts down, I return to the place that I saw during Pain Endurance. The white room never changes. It's always a perfect circle, always pulling me into the epicenter. The object beneath the black blanket in the middle remains a mystery to me. Each time I try to uncover what lies within, I'm pulled back to consciousness, feeling frustrated. I've never wanted answers more.

What is happening to me? Does it mean something? It feels like it does. I've always had one purpose in my life - to serve my country, to kill Inferiors, to build the future for my people. But now, some part of me believes that my purpose lies in the white room. I'm so close to it in my sleep, but when I wake, I have no idea how to go about looking for it. It makes me dread sleep and crave it at the same time. It makes me long for something I've never had, a place I've never been, like homesickness in the loneliness of outer space. But the further I seem from my destination, the more it tears me up that I can't reach it.

I sit up on my bunk, trying to push down the desperate longing inside me. I wipe sleep from my eyes and look around. The room is full, but everyone is quiet. Downtime has been unbearable these last few weeks, and following our performance in the combat simulation, no one is talking. Minnie is lying on her bed sulking. Zach and Ronan are sitting side by side on one of the top bunks, but not speaking, and Marcia is biting her nails on her bed. I have no idea where my brother is, and I'm glad of it. He's the last person I want to see.

These are the people I'm supposed to lead, but I can't lead a disjointed group. This is a nightmare. I thought that unseating Elliott from his throne would be good for all of us, but the resentment bubbling under the surface is evident to me. Zach sees that I'm awake and eyes me up with heat blazing inside him. I guess he always thought he was second best to Elliott, that he would take up his role if anything ever happened to him. I know he's jealous that Captain Strauss picked me to lead instead. And now I'm beginning to question why she bothered. All it's done is give me an impossible task of rescuing our team from drowning.

The quiet and cold stares from my team unnerve me to the point where I stand up and leave the room. There aren't many places we're allowed to go unsupervised in the Institute, and I don't like to break the rules, but I do have a hiding spot where I go occasionally when the world just seems too much.

The rooftop of our building doesn't have much of a view, but it's one of the few places here where it's possible to get any air. If we're not out on the training yard, we're confined to indoors. Even the roof has netting covering it, stopping anything getting in and anything getting out. I suppose it's a safety measure for us, but even though this is home, it does sometimes start to feel claustrophobic. It almost makes me excited to leave here, to go out and start the mission I was born to complete.

Sometimes, I come up here to dream of the future. I think about all the ways in which the oncoming war will improve our lives, and it gives me peace in my heart. The Institute was never meant to feel like a place to settle. I know there's more out there if we're ready to go and take it.

But there are other things on my mind these days too. Namely, the dreams I've been having. I close my eyes and I'm back in that white room, about to uncover what's beneath the blanket. I can't shake it off no matter how I try. Now that I'm awake, I miss the feeling of being electrified, brought to life by the sensations of the dream, but with more questions than answers each time.

I don't understand what is happening to me, what is happening to my body. I feel like I'm going through some kind of rebirth. When I first came here and began to take the X drug, it kind of felt this way, but this is a new level. I feel capable of so much more than I used to be. Despite our poor performance in the combat simulator, I'm at the top of my game. I wonder if the others around me have noticed. Perhaps that's why they're pushing back against me, afraid of what I might be capable of. Before, I was nothing to them. And now, I have strength and agility and focus that they could only dream of. I have power sizzling at my fingertips as though they might burst into flames. I'm not stupid and I know that's impossible. But at the same time, I feel like there's no other explanation.

I feel invincible.

I walk to the edge of the roof, as far as the border will allow me to go. The netting holds me back from the dramatic drop, but as I peer down, I wonder what it would be like to jump. Right now, it doesn't feel like I'd fall.

It feels like I'd fly.

I take a step back, shaking my head to myself. I wish I could shake these thoughts off entirely. What's the matter with me? I've never been cocksure like this before. I've been quietly confident in my abilities, as I should be, but it's reckless to feel this way. It's reckless to believe I'm more than I am. But some urge inside me is telling me that I'm better than the rest. Better than anyone.

I'm jolted from my indulgent thoughts by the sound of the roof door opening. I feel a chill down my spine. Not many people come up here, considering it's not really allowed. Whoever it is must be feeling bold. Or it could be one of the few others who I know comes up here regularly. I've met him on the stairwell a fair few times.

"I hope you're happy. I bet you fucking are. Snake."

I turn and see my brother standing behind me. He always had the kind of rage inside him that he couldn't contain. I can see it in his stance, feet apart, fists curled, chin lowered closer to his chest as he glowers at me. Somehow, it makes me feel calm. At least some things don't change.

"That's nice of you, Elliott. I never thought you had much interest in my happiness."

"You've turned them all against me. You've ruined everything I built here."

I fold my arms. "I didn't do anything at all, Elliott. You dug yourself into this hole. And since we're talking alone, I might as well say that you deserve it. You've put me through hell for years, and for what? I never wanted what you had. I never tried to take anything from you. I just wanted to belong. How does it feel to be in my shoes?"

Elliott kicks at the ground, scuffing his shoes against the floor. At first, I think he might be considering my point. But then he just glares at me again, his blue eyes blazing.

"I worked every damn day of my life to be here. I didn't just walk in and get everything handed to me. Not like *you,*" Elliott says, his voice shaking with rage. "So what if I had to step on your back to get there? You did it to me."

"Hardly. How could I use you as a rung when you weren't even on the ladder? You were sick, Elliott. There was nothing I could do about that. I came here to make the money that treated you. So you're welcome, I guess. Not that I get any gratitude for it. Funnily enough, leaving home as a child to come here was never my dream."

"No, you're right. It was mine. And you took it."

I shake my head, rubbing my fingers against my temple. "You really are *so* blind to what's in front of you, Elliott. How can you blame *me* for this? I tried to be there for you, all these years I would've fought by your side if you asked me to. But you've never stopped pushing me away. I would have helped you when you wanted to join the Institute. But you wouldn't let me."

"I didn't need help. I told you, I made it here by myself."

"Out of choice. You know there's nothing wrong with getting help, Elliott. You've always been so damn proud, but I was here the whole time. For you, I was *always* here," I tell him. I hate the way my voice cracks as I say it. I hate the way that nothing I say matters to him and never has. Has he ever had any love in his heart for me? Does he still cling to the way things used to be, before the Institute, before he got sick, before we lost ourselves entirely to this place?

I don't think it's possible. The way he looks at me now, there's no shred of pain in his eyes, no longing for the past. I don't think he's even capable of loving me. But he smiles, a wolfish look in his gaze.

He's ready to strike a killing blow.

"As far as I'm concerned, Karissa, you're nothing to me. I don't need family. I don't need you, or Mum, or Dad. I made my own family here, but since you took that from me, I'm happy to do this alone. I don't need you, okay? I never have and never will. I don't *want* you. I don't care if we're related by blood. I don't *care* if we shared the womb together. You're nothing but an obstacle in my way."

I don't know how his words can still have the ability to hurt me, but they do. They cut me down to the bone. It's not as though he's saying something I don't know already - if I ever truly had a brother, I lost him a long time ago. But maybe some part of me hoped that we could make up for lost time. That there might still be some kindness left inside him.

I was wrong.

"Alright," I say, jutting my chin out. "If that's the way you want it. From now on, we'll do things your way. I'm sick and tired of pretending you're not a monster. I won't take any responsibility for you any longer. And considering that I've always been dead to you, I guess it's time I killed the last bit of hope I had for us." I step up toward him, my whole body shaking with anger, but I won't back down. We're almost butting heads as I square up to him.

"If I were you, I'd watch your fucking back," I whisper. "Because I'm not doing it for you any longer. And guess what?" I lower my voice another level. "Everyone you love is sharpening their knives to stab you right between your shoulders."

RAVEN

My whole body is aching by the time we get back to the school. I can feel the place on my back where the baton beat me down. My stomach feels tender and sore, like it does when I get my period, but ten times worse. I sat quietly the whole journey, not wanting to bring attention to it, especially with Roger watching my every move. But the physical pain is bringing tears to my eyes and the emotions of what I just went through aren't helping.

But we all made it back in one piece. That was the goal. We've brought back supplies that will feed hundreds of hungry mouths for a few more days. It has to be worth it. I have to take this as a success.

I wince as Logan opens the back doors to the van and I try to hop down to the pavement.

"Let me help you," he says. Roger smirks as he jumps down. No one else seems to notice his cruel response to my pain. Is it in my mind? I shake my head.

"I'm okay. We need to get the supplies inside."

I try not to let the pain get to me as we take the food to the canteen. A group of cooks has banded together, taking it upon themselves to cook hot meals for the survivors here every night. They seem pleased with what we've managed to grab which makes me feel a little better.

"You don't look so good, Raven," June says gently, cupping my cheek. The gesture is so motherly that it takes me by surprise. It makes me think of my own mom and tears sting my eyes even harder. I swallow back my emotions.

"I'm okay. Some rest will help."

"Take it easy," Ellis says. For the first time, she doesn't have anything negative to add. I nod to her. Maybe this is the start of a friendship for us.

"Let's go find Jonah, hmm?" Logan says, slinging an arm around my shoulder and guiding me to the main part of the building. "We've done enough for one day."

"Don't tell him what happened, okay?" I warn Logan. "He doesn't need to know."

"He's your brother, Raven. He'll be able to tell something's up. Besides...don't take this the wrong way, but you can't protect him from everything. I know he's a kid, but this might be a good chance to show him that he needs to grow up. If he's going to make it-"

"He doesn't need to know. And nothing's going to happen to him. He's going to make it because I'll make sure he does," I snap. I know it's nowhere near that simple, but I don't like the way Logan's talking. As our hips bump together, his pocket crackles. I frown. He's obviously keeping something in there. Right now, though, I don't question it. I'm too concerned with keeping the pain from showing on my face.

Walking up seven flights of stairs proves to be a strain I wasn't expecting. It makes the pain seem even more severe than before. The sooner these bruises heal, the better. I pause for breath and catch sight of something through a doorway that interests me. I peer through the glass, feeling a smile forming on my face.

Jonah is sitting listening to an older woman talk. She's pointing at a whiteboard that has the alphabet on it. The kids in the room are younger than Jonah, but he's listening intently anyway, eager to learn.

"He's at school," I whisper. Logan peers into the room too with a chuckle.

"Looks like some good has come out of this whole mess at least."

I'm grinning ear to ear. Only days ago I thought we were being served a death sentence. Now, Jonah can do things he never did before. Play with other kids, learn from a real adult, have a life that's actually worth living. There's still pain in my bones, but I know it's more than worth it now. This is what I should be fighting for.

"We should go back downstairs. I was thinking earlier, maybe we can take the van and your ration cards a little further tomorrow. We should-"

"-we should do something about your bruising," Logan tells me softly. He reaches in his pocket and brings out a square package. "I got us an ice pack to reduce the swelling. I've got pills back in the office too. For the pain."

"Logan, we shouldn't be keeping that kind of stuff to ourselves."

"You risked your life today for every single person in this building. You can at least tend to the bruising or you'll be fit for nothing. Come on. Upstairs."

I roll my eyes, but he's right. The way I'm feeling right now, I can't do much for anyone. Logan gently guides me up another two flights of stairs to where the headmaster's office is. Logan moves to the bookshelves and reaches behind a set of folders, producing a packet of pills.

"What else do you have behind there?"

"A few medical supplies. A spare knife. A book."

"A book?"

Logan smiles. "I picked it up for you a few years ago. I thought you'd like the story. I guess I just never got the chance to give it to you."

"Can I have it now?" I say with a smile. He folds his arms.

"After you let me ice your bruise. You'll need to change your top. Ice packs shouldn't go directly on the skin."

I don't even try to argue. He turns so that I can take off my ridiculous outfit and put on my threadbare vest. I try to ignore the shoots of pain through my back, telling myself the pain is all in my head, but it's enough to make me grind my teeth hard. I watch as Logan snaps the ice pack and peers at my back. He winces.

"It's bad?"

"That guy beat the shit out of you, Raven. I'm so sorry."

"It's not your fault."

"I didn't even notice what was happening. I was too busy running away."

"You stuck to the plan."

Logan sighs as he presses the pack to my bruises. I wince, but say nothing.

"I'd never knowingly leave you behind, Raven. I know I wouldn't be much use in a fight. I mean, if you're losing a fight then adding me to the equation won't solve things. You're the tough one out of us. But I'd come back anyway. That's why I'm sorry I didn't. I should've been looking out for you."

I think about what Roger said earlier about Logan checking up on me every few minutes. Seems like he was right. I sigh.

"Look, Logan...don't feel guilty. No one knows how they'd react in a moment like that. Your instincts kick in and you don't know what they'll make you do. It took me a long time and a lot of fights to force myself to resist that urge to run. You learn to protect yourself, but also other people over time."

Logan pauses for a moment, completely silent. Then he sighs.

"We come from different worlds, huh?"

"You're just realizing that now?"

"I guess so. In truth, Raven...I never thought too hard about the life you lead. I never saw you outside of my own world, you know? It's like watching a TV programme...you don't know what happens off-screen."

I don't mention that I've never actually watched anything on TV. Not unless doomsday political screenings count. Logan shifts the ice pack and I wince.

"You've never had any reason to want to know about my life. It's not pretty, so what's the point in you suffering through it too?"

"Because I want to be wherever you are. Even when times are hard. I know things look bleak now...I know I've stepped away from the life I could've had. But I don't care about that. I've found you again. That's what is important to me."

"So you're not scared?"

"Oh, I'm scared. I spend every minute of every day wondering when this will all fall apart. I find myself thinking about all the things that could go wrong, all the ways me and my friends might die on any given day. I know there are no guarantees, and if we make a mistake, there are no second chances. But it's worth it."

I glance over my shoulder at him and he smiles at me gently. He really believes what he's saying to me. He lays his spare hand on my shoulder and I almost shiver. I don't want him to go anywhere. Selfishly, I want him to stay and endure this whole nightmare with me.

"It just feels strange to me," I tell him. "I've always known how it would be to live your life...at least I could imagine it...but now you're living mine. And even though I thought you wouldn't be able to handle it...it kind of works. You fit into this scenario."

Logan smiles. "I'm trying. I guess it's taking some getting used to. Earlier my heart was pounding so hard I thought I was going to be sick. But I'm here to stay. And listen to me...you don't have to struggle so hard anymore. I know the past four years have been hard on you. You've had so much responsibility and so little support. But consider me your partner now. I'm going to do everything I can to help you. I'll help you care for Jonah. I'll tend to you if you get hurt again.

I'll be with you in every fight. Hell, say the word and I'll rub your feet."

I grin. "Even after I've been wearing my smelly boots?"

He grins back. "Even then. I promise, no matter what you need me for, I've got your back. And next time we need to fight, I'm staying right next to you."

I close my eyes and try not to smile. It feels like such a long time since someone tried to take care of me. My mother was always there for me when she was alive and well, but after she lost her job, it started to feel like I was the one taking care of her. I didn't mind. I'd have done anything for her. But with no one to care for me, I felt the weight of the world pressing down on my shoulders every day.

But now Logan's here. I know in my heart he'd do anything for me. I don't know if that's out of love or guilt for what his father did, but either way, he means every word of his promise. He'd live and die for me because that's the kind of man he is. I'd never want to exploit that, but it feels so good to have someone who cares for me.

I want to rest my head against his chest and close my eyes. I want to feel his arms wrapped around me and allow myself to rest for the first time in years. But the moment I let my guard down too much, I'll start making mistakes that I can't afford. Logan has - and always will be - my weakness. That means keeping him at arm's length, even when every instinct I have is telling me to draw him closer.

"Hopefully this should have helped with the swelling," Logan says as he removes the ice pack from my back. He hands me his water bottle and a few pills from his pocket. "For the pain."

"Thank you," I tell him, ignoring the warmth that's filling my heart. As I take the pills, I think about the book he kept for me. I desperately want to know what it is. I want him to spend the evening reading it to me the way he used to at his father's parties. But that kind of intimacy is dangerous. It puts my heart on the line. So since he seems to have forgotten about it for now, I won't ask about it again.

It's better this way.

Down in the canteen, the smell of cooking is making my stomach rumble. Me and Logan were invited with the rest of the council to take the first servings of food this evening as a reward for our work, but it feels wrong to me. Jonah is all too happy to be at the front of the queue with me, peering at the serving dishes that the catering staff have laid out, but discomfort is sitting in my stomach.

"I'm not sure about this," I admit aloud. "Some of these people haven't eaten for days. Why should we get served first?"

"Someone has to be at the front of the line," Roger says. His arm is wrapped around his boyfriend's waist. Drew is scrawny and has a mop of brown curls on his head, similar to Jonah's. He hasn't spoken or looked in our direction since we got here. "Why not us, Raven? You got used as a punching bag today and you don't think you deserve to get served first?"

I squirm in discomfort. I'm not used to this kind of thing. I've always been selfish in terms of putting food on the table. Back at home, I'd steal from people who had little more than I did. I'd fight for scraps if necessary. But now, looking behind me and seeing so many solemn faces, caved inward by starvation, it feels harder to justify putting myself above them. June is standing behind me and she rubs my shoulder gently.

"Don't overthink it," she says, "You've done well today. You're not taking food out of anyone's mouth. Without you, they wouldn't be eating at all. They just have to wait their turn. I'm sure you've done your fair share of waiting in the past."

I sigh. I know she's right, in a way. And I want Jonah to be able to eat without me making a big deal out of this. But I can't stop the guilt from overtaking me. As we shuffle forward to collect our dinner, I'm served a steaming portion of rice and vegetables. It feels like a luxury and the smell makes my stomach hurt in anticipation. Yet still, it feels wrong.

I sit with the others to eat, but while the others begin to shovel food into their mouths, I can't stop watching people lining up for their dinner. I can see some people bent double in pain and I know what they're experiencing - the kind of hunger that makes you feel like you're going to die.

Further down the line, the scuffles have begun. People are pushing forward, trying to make the queue go faster. People are trying their hardest not to give in to those who are shoving their way forward, but with no one to keep the line in order, the tension is palpable.

And this can only get worse. We might have a hot meal today, but what about tomorrow, and all the days that follow? We're going to run out of supplies. We're going to slowly lose people to starvation and disease and exhaustion. I'm coming to the awful realization that this is as good as it gets. Nothing is promised.

"Eat up, Raven," Roger says darkly. "You never know when your last meal might be."

RILEY

I've heard that it's not becoming to count your money, but I've never had much interest in manners. I sit with my friends and we stuff handfuls of cash into our pockets from our latest winnings. It's been a good few nights at the casino. We've had the occasional loss, but I stuck to my plan, heading to the tables where nothing much ever happens and the losers don't expect anything less. I've been slowly stacking up my money, making out like a bandit with their cash. It's given me a buzz in my veins like I'm on drugs or something. It makes me feel like maybe I made some right choices along the way. Like maybe I can get me and my friends out of here, to somewhere better. Maybe we can have a life worth living.

We're sitting in a circle, the four of us still camped outside the casino. It's not so bad out here if you can overlook the sounds of rioting in the night. Sometimes there's gunfire, but there have been whisperings about people in gray jumpsuits acting nuts as they run around the streets looking barely human. I wonder if the guns are aimed at them, or at the ordinary people fighting for their lives. I wish I could tell them there are smarter ways to try and win their lives back. That they're only going to get themselves killed by throwing themselves at people with guns and government backing. But the words would be wasted considering most of them are about to die anyway.

So the four of us try to forget what we can hear and focus on what we can see. Wads of cash and soup from the kitchens next door to the casino. We have a hunk of bread each to pad it out. We're trying to be sensible, knowing that the X drug is going to cost us an arm and a leg. Not to mention the fact that we're probably going to have to pay someone to forge us some ID. As far as the government knows, none of us exist. We all grew up poor, unable to register ourselves as citizens because we never had the money. Never had rations cards, never had enough cash to buy anything but the essentials. We all worked from a young age instead of going to school, helping our parents to keep us alive. Some life that was. Now, as the soup warms my stomach, I feel a little better. At least we have some control over our future now. So long as we keep this up, we're going to be fine.

"Excuse me…could you spare a mouthful of bread?"

I look up and see a weedy boy standing over us. He looks terrified to be talking to us, but he's reaching out a grubby hand to accept whatever he thinks we might offer. I almost turn him away. I've never been in a position to give out free handouts before, and no one has ever given them to me. But the kid looks like he's one day away from collapse, and I don't want to be responsible for that. I tear off a hunk of my bread and hand it to him.

"Here. Don't scoff it all at once," I say, raising an eyebrow. Slowly, a smile forms on his face and he holds the bread close to his chest like he's hugging it.

"Thank you. Thank you so much."

"Don't mention it. I mean literally, don't. We can't have every street rat running to us wanting a bit of something," I say. I expect him to walk away now, but he hovers around, like he's waiting for something else. Elianna eyes him up carefully before her eyes soften a little.

"Do you want to join us?"

"Yes please," the boy says immediately, dropping down to our level and crossing his legs. I'm not sure how I feel about having him with us. He's a bit odd, but then aren't we all, I suppose? I watch him gnaw at the bread, his eyes wide as he does. He's weirding me out so I look away again.

"What's your name, kid?" Squid asks him.

"Wally," he responds with a big grin on his face. Squid snorts.

"What kind of name is that?"

"Says the guy we call Squid," I remind him with a grin. It never felt right to call him by his real name after we left the Pits. Same with Tiger. Elianna always hated her nickname, but for the rest of us, the nicknames were fun. They gave us a sense of belonging. I miss when they used to call me Phoenix, too. Riley just doesn't have the same vibe to it.

"My mum knew a guy once called Walter…she said he taught her how to survive this city. Named me after him," Wally said. Tiger chews his thumb.

"Where is she now?"

Wally continues to gnaw at his bread. "She died. When the government announcement was made…she got caught in a scrum. I saw her go down."

"I'm so sorry," Elianna says gently.

"It's alright. She's somewhere better now. I kind of wish I'd gone with her. I hardly know what to do with myself."

"Well, join the club," Squid says with his attempt at a sympathetic smile. "We've got a whole lot of nothing between the four of us. We're just scraping by."

"How did you afford…this?" Wally asks, gesturing to the meager serving of food before us as though it's a damn feast.

"We earned it. Fighting in the Pits," I tell him. "And we're going to try our hand at the casinos and win some more."

"Cool," Wally says, grinning dopily again. "Nothing to lose anymore, is there? We may as well do what we can with our time."

I catch Tiger watching Wally with unease. I don't know what his problem is. Wally is worse off than us. But I tend to trust Tiger's judgment most of the time. He's quiet, but he's always had good instincts. They've kept him alive. It makes me question whether we should be being so open with this stranger. But he's just a kid. Not much older than me. What harm can he be when he's scoffing a hunk of bread down like he's never eaten before in his life?

He sighs as he finishes his bread, picking crumbs off of his trousers. His stomach gurgles. "Thanks for the food," he says, rubbing his stomach. "I think I really needed that."

"You can set up camp with us if you like. But we're heading into the casino now. We won't be sticking around here. Best to spend the nights indoors if we can," Squid says. Wally grins again.

"I'll hold your spot for you. You've got prime real estate here, guys. You wouldn't want to lose it."

I snort. "Funny. Alright, you can hold our spot. And here, finish up my soup. You look like you need it."

I hand my bowl to him and stand up, brushing the crumbs of my bread onto the floor. I've got big plans for tonight in the casino. I'm moving on to some of the bigger tables where the blinds are bigger, but the prize pot is huge. A few more days here and we might be ready to get out for good.

"Good luck! Hope you win!" Wally calls after us.

"Aww. Nice kid," Squid says cheerily as we head inside. I don't have time to think about Wally anymore. It's time to get focussed and start winning some money.

It's past midnight. I've already made some serious money this evening. I'm sitting at a poker table with a sour faced woman dealing the cards, her hair scraped back on her head so hard it must hurt. The players around this table are dull and harder to play with than the likes of Eros, but they're offering up bigger rewards, and I can't turn that down.

I roll my shoulders back. An ache is settling into my bones. The place where Bull stabbed me throbs almost constantly and I'm tired. The thrill I first felt coming here has quickly waned. Now I just want this to be over with so we can set up someplace new. Just a little while longer. Just a few more risks until I can live my life in peace.

One of the players gets up from the table and walks away, her chips firmly placed in my large pile. I've definitely played the best tonight, and it shows. Most of this lot will give up soon and I'll have to find another table, but there's no sense in running away from a game I'm winning.

But a new player is joining us now. I watch as a young man with scruffy brown hair seats himself opposite me and my eyebrows knit together as I recognize him.

"Wally? What the hell are you doing here?"

He smiles and somehow, I can see an entirely new person in front of me. He's not smiling like he's a street kid begging for bread. He's smiling like a kid who knows exactly what he's doing. I take in the fact that he's scrubbed clean, wearing a fresh shirt without any crinkles in it.

Something tells me I've been fooled.

"I thought I'd take my chances on one of the games," Wally said pleasantly. Then he produces a large stack of chips from his pocket. My heart is beating a little faster. Something feels off.

"I thought you didn't have any money?"

"I didn't. Just kind of lucked out today on one of the games," Wally says. "They were allowing free bets on the roulette table. I guess it must have been meant to be."

I still don't feel much better about having him here. It feels wrong. But the cards are being dealt and it's too late to turn back now. I pick up my cards and take a look. Could be worse. An eight and a Queen. Wally looks at his cards too and I try to read his face. I don't care much about the other players at the table now that he's here. I wonder what his game is. He didn't seem streetwise enough for poker when I met him earlier. And all of a sudden he's here by luck? Doesn't seem right to me.

The game moves forward. The blinds are paid and the first three cards turn over. I barely blink at the formation. A King, an eight and a two. This is a decent start for me. I raise a little just to weed out some of the other players. I'm not surprised when Wally matches me. I wish I could read his face better. It makes me miss playing against Eros. But the stakes are higher at this table, and I've already got a pair. If I can find something better, I could be in with a shot at some money here.

Four players remain. The next card is turned over. I watch it turn and my heart skips a beat. King of Hearts. I've got two pairs now. Another eight or a King and I'll have a full house. It doesn't seem out of the realms of possibility. I throw in another few chips and the other two players at the table immediately withdraw. Wally holds steady, matching me casually. I wonder what he's got. Either he has nothing and he's stupid enough to make risky plays, or he has something good. I guess we'll see.

The next card turns. I resist a smile. Another King. Three Kings on the table is a rarity, but there are a million ways the cards can fall. I push my nerves aside and raise a little further. A full house is a good hand, there's no denying that. And an eight is high, so if Wally has a full house too then I'll beat him unless he has an eight too. There's not much else he could do with his hand. I doubt he'll have four of a kind. How often does that ever come up?

Wally seems to be debating what to do, drumming his fingers on the table. Maybe I've pushed him too far. It's tempting to smile, but I won't. It feels like tempting bad luck. Besides, I don't want to see him lose. In theory, he's in the same shoes as me. I don't want to take him down. Even if his damn smile is getting on my nerves now.

I watch as he makes his move. He uses the edge of his arm to push all of his chips forward. My heart squeezes. Surely not?

"All in," he says with a decisive nod. I stare at his pile of chips. I imagine what I could do with that kind of money. The cards in my hand are almost a sure bet of a win. The odds of him having something better are next to zero. A straight flush isn't possible…can I do this? Can I take it all from him?

I know that my friends are watching me, probably screaming inside for me not to do it. But I feel my arm move almost involuntarily, pushing a matching amount of chips forward. It's not everything I have, but it's a lot of it. But where's the risk when the odds are stacked way in my favor? This isn't a round I should lose. It's almost impossible. There's only one card that can win him the game.

"Show your hand," the dealer says. I go first. I put down my cards.

"A full house," I say quietly. My heart is thumping in my ears. I feel sick. Why am I so scared? I've got this in the bag.

But Wally is smiling and it's scaring me.

He lays his cards down in front of him. My heart sinks to my stomach. I stare at him, wondering what the hell just happened.

"Five of a kind," he murmurs, looking me dead in the eye. On the table, he's laid out a king and a joker. A wild card. No one told me there was a joker in the pack. This shouldn't have been possible. I turn to the dealer, rage filling me to the brim, but she smirks to herself and it suddenly becomes clear. This was always going to happen. The cards were rigged.

I was set up to lose.

"No," I whisper. I'm frozen in place as Wally rakes in my pile of chips from the table. I'm watching him take everything from me in one fell swoop. "No, the game is void. You didn't tell us there were wild cards in the pack."

"Doesn't matter. He's got four of a kind even without the joker. He beat you either way."

"Is this some kind of sick joke? You rigged these cards, I know it. I want my money back!"

"The game's over, kid. Let it go. You lost," the dealer tells me. I want to wipe that stupid grin off her face. But more than that, I want to destroy Wally for what he did to me. It's clear to me now that this was always his plan - butter me up and then take me down. After we gave him food from our stash, after we took care of him…he was leading up to this. He knew what he was going to do. He knew he was going to come here, cheat at the game and then take everything from me. Someone put him up to this, I'm sure of it. And he accepted, knowing what it would do to me.

I want to kill him.

"No!" I cry out. The anger is overspilling and I can't contain it any longer. I try to run at Wally, to grab him by the neck, but someone stops me. A meaty hand holds me back easily and I look up to see a bouncer keeping me at bay. It's like he was planted nearby, knowing this would happen. While I was busy playing poker, the casino was playing chess, preparing to check the reigning king of the table.

"No fighting," the bouncer says through gritted teeth. I hiss at the boy who took everything from me, his smile still easy and calm as though nothing ever happened here.

"You have a no cheating policy too. I suppose that goes out of the window when you're all taking a cut of the money, huh? When you're all walking away with cash in your pocket what do we matter, huh? Is that how you want to play it? I can fight dirty too."

I bite straight into the bouncer's arm and he yelps, letting me go long enough to give me one final chance at launching myself at Wally. The bouncer grabs me again and hauls me back, but I watch as a red sleeve reaches out and stops him. I look up, my cheeks hot. The woman in the crimson coat. The woman I saw when I first arrived here. She must have as much power as I suspected, because everyone freezes in place at her command.

"Leave her. She'll behave, won't you?" she says with a pointed look at me. The fire in me douses just a little, despite my fury. I suddenly realize that she must have orchestrated this. She must have seen me playing the field and wanted to catch me out. She saw me climbing the ladder and had to find a way to knock me off.

She played the game, and she played it better than me.

But she watches me steadily now, daring me to make another false move. She's giving me a chance to walk away with my life, if nothing else. Everything inside me is making me want to fight some more. But I could get myself killed in a place like this. I could get my friends killed. I stop struggling and take a step back. The woman nods.

"Good," she said. She turns to Wally. "Congratulations on your win, sir. Perhaps you might take your winnings and go now."

"Absolutely," Wally says with a warm smile. He looks back at me again, his lips quirking in amusement. "If I see you again, I'll be sure to toss you some scraps."

My hands curl into fists. He's trying to get a rise out of me and it's damn well working. I watch him walk away with almost everything I have. I'm shaking. I turn and see my friends watching me in shock. But not just shock. Hurt. Anger. Frustration. I start towards them, wishing I could explain what I've figured out, but Elianna storms away, trying to get away from me. I rush to her, still not processing what has just happened, and grab her wrist. She whirls around to face me.

"Don't touch me, Riley."

"So don't walk away from me!"

"Why shouldn't I? You just cost us everything!"

"You're overreacting. It's not *all* gone. I'll win it back. I'll make it right," I say. I wonder if the desperation in my voice is obvious. Elianna clenches her jaw, staring into my eyes with the kind of fire I've always had in me, but never seen in her. She's always been like water, cooling me off whenever I run too hot. Now the tables have turned. I've never seen her this angry before.

"I warned you to be careful, but you refused to listen to me. You always think you know better. And now look at what's happened. We're left with nothing again."

"You had nothing anyway! We all knew that the money we had wouldn't be enough to save us all."

"Yes, we did know that! But we tried to give that money to you, Riley! And now you don't have any either. Don't you see what you've done? Every time we follow your ideas, it only causes trouble. Look at Eagle. Look at Bull! They're both dead, and for what? You squandered the money you won in the Pit, and now we're all dead."

The twisting in my stomach is ugly and hot. She's right, of course. I killed Bull to get that money. And now that it's gone, I realize we could've both walked away with our lives. Maybe not for very long, but Bull would still be with us now if I hadn't suggested the match. Maybe she'd be right here in this gambling hall with me, knocking back overpriced whiskey and having a laugh. Enjoying this little life we have left while we can.

But I ended her life. I took away her chances, and I fucked up my own. Now none of us have anything. But I can't admit that out loud. I'm too proud. And since Bull's blood is on my hands, I can't allow them to think this was all for nothing.

That shame might kill me.

"Well if you're so damn smart, you tell me what you would've done differently!" I snap, eyeing Elianna up with the same venom she injected into her own gaze. "You've always done well at standing on the sidelines and telling me how to live. Who was the one who trained you to stay alive in the Pits, huh? Who was the one who tried to find a way to keep us all in with a chance when the Pits shut down? Who is the one who has been busting her butt to make us rich? Because it damn sure isn't you. It's always been me. You whine and complain at me as though I'm not the reason you're alive. You'd be useless without me."

Elianna presses her lips into a thin line. I've taken it too far, but I'm the queen of doing that. She stares me down, shaking her head slowly.

"Maybe you should've just let me die then. Because I don't like you like this. I don't like the world like this. Maybe it just wasn't meant for me."

She walks away from me before I can find words to say. I love her like a sister and I hate her like one too. But in this moment, I feel so detached from her that I wonder if we can ever be right again. How can she say such things? After everything we've done to stay alive? After everything I've given from inside myself to her, to Tiger, to Squid?

A piece of me died that last day in the Pits. The part of me that had any hope for this world. But I'm still fighting. I won't stop because if I do, and this turns out to be for nothing, then how can I ever live with myself?

I roll back my shoulders and lift my chin up high. I walk over to the bar and find Squid there, hunched over a drink. His eyes are heavy and he manages a weak smile, raising his glass to me.

"It's on the house, apparently. Considering we're the biggest losers in England."

"Hey, that's not true. At least we're not those poor suckers who died on the first night, right? We've got some days left in us. Come on, I'm not going down just yet. And if I am, I plan to be drunk when I do."

Squid laughs and pushes the glass toward me. Then he ruffles my short hair. "I don't know how the hell you do it, kid. The world stays sunny when you're in it."

I don't say what I want to say. I want to tell him that I'm not sunny, I *am* the sun. I'm a blazing ball of fire with red hair and enough anger in me to keep me burning long after everyone else has turned to ashes. And even when I'm done burning, I'll rise from those ashes and be reborn again, the phoenix that just won't bloody die.

Even when everything else is lost.

RAVEN

The lights went out today at the school. So did the gas and the water. We don't have working appliances anymore. No heating. No fresh water to bathe in or drink.

We knew this was coming, of course. Now that the riots have almost slowed to a halt, the government is finding ways to turn their backs on the rest of us. Someone must have told them about all the refugees holed up here and now they're done with giving us a free ride.

Will they come here and shoot the place up? I doubt it. It's bad for their image. It's bad enough that they've handed us all a death sentence without them pulling the trigger too. No, I think they'll wait it out. They know where we are now and they know how little we have. The food supply is running low now. I haven't eaten in three days so I can give my rations to Jonah and keep him strong. It's getting harder to steal and the food we've been growing is barely enough to feed a family.

Things are going to hell.

Besides, they've got their secret weapon at hand too. As the riots subside and the protestors lie dead in the streets, the feral humans have been closing in on our perimeter. So far, we've managed to keep them out, but sometimes at night, I hear them. They scream and claw at the walls while we try to save precious bullets by fighting them hand to hand. People have died protecting this place, though no one talks about it. New fighters join the ranks with empty stomachs and fear in their hearts. Even Lark can't joke about the things he's seen while protecting the wall from them.

It's evening time. This is when the gray jumpsuiters tend to strike. Another evening without a meal, and the first evening when hot food hasn't been available. I know tonight will be tough.

I'm sitting in the office with Jonah snuggled close to me for warmth. The blanket we brought with us is a lifeline now. If it's cold now, what will it be like in winter? If we make it that far, that is. This building wasn't made for a crisis like this.

I look up as Theodore and Logan enter the room. They've got mud on their hands so I know they've been out tending to the gardens again. Theodore offers me a smile and I try to smile back.

"Those tomatoes seem to be growing well," he says, rubbing his hands together. I can't tell if he's trying to warm them up or rid them of the dirt on his hands.

"You'll have a whole tomato farm in no time," I say brightly.

Logan doesn't look like he's in the mood for jokes. Neither am I, truth be told, but this whole thing is hitting him harder. He doesn't know how to live like this.

Someone's stomach groans. I can remember being at a party at Logan's once and the sound of a hungry stomach made him and his friends laugh. They spent a few minutes imitating the groaning noises of a tummy and laughing about it. No one's laughing now.

Theodore produces a pack of cards from his pockets and he teaches us all some games to keep our minds off the world outside. It works for a while, but when Jonah falls asleep on the sofa, Logan and Theodore fall solemn again. I stand up and look out of the window. The windows are pretty soundproof, but I see the street light up with machine gun fire. That can only mean there are more jumpsuiters at the perimeter.

"What do they want?" I ask.

"I'm not sure they want anything. Maybe that's the point of them," Theodore says. "They run off their impulses."

I imagine the kind of person it must take to create a drug that sends people so wild that they don't even seem human anymore. Those creatures outside are capable of ripping out throats with their teeth, tearing people open with their rabid hands, beating people so viciously with their fists that their bones break. Perhaps we all have that ability in us, but we've never once had the drive. It's a sickening thought that one wrong move will remove the barrier between us and them.

I can't help wondering about the people outside of the walls. Wren might still be out there somewhere. I've looked around every day, hoping she might have made it to the school, but I still haven't seen her. Maybe her family is actually eligible for the X drug. After all, their meat van is a good earner. But if she's out there...scared and alone…

It's unthinkable.

And now these things are on our doorstep. I don't think we can't hold them off forever. And when they get in, no one will make it out unharmed.

"What are we doing here?" I whisper. "This isn't safe anymore. It's just scary. There must be somewhere else to go…"

"We're in one of the densest cities in the country. They don't tell you that when you live somewhere like this...but we have one of the biggest populations of any city in the country," Theodore tells me. "Maybe it is safer elsewhere. Where there's less people, that is. But we've waited too long. Now that the rioting has died down...all eyes will be on us. We leave here and we're fair game for the police...think of the crimes we've committed to get us this far."

"The real crime is that they want us dead...for their *convenience,*" I hiss. I can feel tears stinging my eyes. Theodore puts an arm around my shoulder.

"I know. And it's easy to give in to anger. But we have to keep our cool. Irrationality is what will fail us now."

I nod, though I'm struggling to stay positive. I don't understand how Theodore does it sometimes. He lost both his parents at a young age. His father was shot for stealing. His mother died of the flu. His adopted parents tried to erase his past and make him act like a rich boy. But he's always felt more like me than any of the others in his group. He understands the struggles ahead of us better than the likes of Logan and Lark.

"Maybe we should have some kind of escape route, though...just in case," I say, wrapping my arms around myself. "If things go crazy here we don't want to get stuck."

It's at this moment that Lark returns from his shift. He's holding something in his hand and grinning.

"Check it out. A few of us raided the kitchens. I brought back the spoils."

I'm horrified when he holds up a box of cereal bars. I recognize them because I'm the one who stole them from the supermarket the other day. I stare at him.

"What is wrong with you?"

Lark's face falls. "Huh?"

"There's rationing for a reason. No wonder food supplies are running low!"

Lark rolls his eyes. "Come on...we all know June and Ellis are going overboard with the rationing. I worked hard today. I want to sit with my friends and eat something proper for once."

"You think you're the only one who worked hard? You think we don't want to do those things too?"

"I brought these for you too! I'm not just eating them by myself..."

"Lark...you know that's not what she was saying," Theodore says gently. "You can't just take food now."

Lark scowls. "I thought you'd be pleased. Raven, you've barely eaten in days."

"Pleased?" I scoff. "You're stealing food from someone else's mouth!"

"Don't be so damn dramatic."

I feel rage surge inside me and I want to launch myself toward him, but Theodore holds me back at the last moment. Logan snatches the box of cereal bars from Lark's hand, his face quietly contorted in anger.

"Enough. We're taking this back to the kitchens. Hopefully no one will catch us doing it. You really need to change your attitude, Lark. We're all hungry. We're all tired. You won't catch the rest of us pulling shit like this."

Lark argues indignantly as he follows Logan down the stairs. I'm quietly shaking with anger.

"He just doesn't get it, does he? Do you think he ever will?"

Theodore sighs. "Who knows. For his sake, I hope so. He's lucky we caught him and not someone else. But if I know him like I think I do, he'll come around. It might not seem like it, but he's learning. Sometimes people just need a handful of second chances to make a change."

"You know who wouldn't get a second chance? People like us. The people who don't have money to throw at a problem," I say, shaking my head. "This is his last chance as far as I'm concerned. I'm tired of sticking to the rules while stupid boys like him think they can get away with anything."

Suddenly, I can hear a commotion on the stairwell. I exchange a glance with Theodore and then run out to see what the issue is.

Lark and Roger are facing off on the stairs. Roger has three of his friends backing him up, while Logan is trying his best to get between Lark and Roger.

"What's going on here?"

Roger looks up the stairwell at me and for the first time, I feel a pang of fear toward him. His eyes hold the kind of fury that makes you feel like you're burning from the inside out when he looks at you. He points an accusatory finger at Lark.

"Your friend has been stealing from the kitchens."

I can feel my heart hammering against my chest. I should've known something like this would happen. Ever since we went to the supermarket, Roger and his friends from his gang have taken it upon themselves to act like some kind of security team. It was agreed by the council that they could have some powers to punish those breaking the rules, which seemed like a good idea at the time, even if it made me uneasy. Now, I'm not so sure.

"We've dealt with it. He's taking the food back right now."

"Once a thief, always a thief, right?" Roger says coldly, glaring at Lark. I feel anger bubbling in me once again. As angry as I am with Lark, Roger is really starting to infuriate me.

"You should know," I snap, thinking of his gang tattoo on his wrist. Roger remains calm, unbothered by my remark. He's a hypocrite and he knows it, but that won't stop him doing what he wants.

"We can't just let people get away with things like this. He should be made an example of. That was what we agreed at the council."

"That wasn't what was agreed," Logan says, trying to keep his voice level. "Reprimanded? Yes. Embarrassed publicly? Absolutely not."

Roger grabs Lark hard by the arm. "Maybe next time he'll think twice about what he takes. Got a problem with it? Take it up with the council."

Roger begins to drag Lark with him down the staircase. Logan doesn't seem to know how to react. I rush down the stairs after them. As angry as I am with Lark, I don't like how Roger is acting.

"What are you going to do?"

Roger stops for a moment and turns to me, his face calm like we're talking about the weather. "A punishment befitting a thief. I'm going to take away what he stole. Three days without rations and isolation should do the trick."

"That's cruel."

"So was his behavior. He had no regard for anyone else...why should we have regard for him?" Roger reasons calmly. He leans a little closer to me. "Between you and me, Raven, I think he needs to see how the other half live. If he's going to sink to our level then maybe he should commit to the experience entirely. The likes of you and me...we know how to go hungry, right?"

"We're not the same," I hiss. I'll never be like Roger. This whole thing has just proved how different our approaches to life are. I might have done bad things to survive, but Roger seeks out trouble. I can see a glint in his eyes and a curve in his charming smile.

He's enjoying this.

"It's happening, Raven. Don't fight me on this one."

"Raven…" Lark protests, his eyes wide. I can see the terror he's experiencing. He's scared to be alone with his thoughts, alone with his fear, alone with the gnawing hunger in his stomach. Who wouldn't be? I grit my teeth.

"I'm calling a council meeting. This is going to be dealt with."

Roger leans in closer still.

"If you have any sense, Raven, you won't cross me," he mutters. Then he drags Lark away, leaving me standing on the stairway and wondering how the hell I'm going to get Lark out of this one.

KARISSA

Captain Strauss called me to her office this morning and I head there now that I've finished my training for the day. There's a new, but familiar buzz carrying me through the days now. I want to ask the Captain if they're changed my dosage, if something is different about the X drug, but I've been trained not to ask questions. If something has changed, then perhaps they're not willing to tell me about it. In some ways, me and my fellow soldiers have always stumbled a little blindly through all of this. We do what we're told because that's what will keep us alive. That's what will help us win the war. Maybe when it's over, we will get the chance to think for ourselves, to do as we please. But for now, I'm a spoke on the wheel. I keep it turning, and it's an honor to do so. Not even our Captain could teach me the unrequited love I have for our people and my desperation to serve them.

Captain Strauss is standing by the window when I enter her office. She turns to me without smiling. I remind myself that she's probably called me here to chastise me. My team is on the brink of a breakdown, after all.

"Have a seat, Soldier. We have a lot to talk about."

I do as she asks. She sits down opposite me and stares at me for a moment, almost sizing me up. Then she sighs back into her seat.

"I've put a big task on your shoulders, Karissa. Turning your team around in your favor was never going to be an overnight job. I appreciate that you're doing the best you can with what you've been given. But put simply, it isn't enough."

I want to hang my head in shame, but I keep my chin up. Captain Strauss would never want to see me give in so easily. "I know. I know that there's a lot I need to work on. If you have any feedback on my performance, I would be glad to take it on board."

Captain Strauss looks amused, though I can't figure out why. She takes a sip from the glass of water on her table, but her eyes never leave me.

"I won't be here to hold your hand forever, Karissa. What do your instincts tell you? What do you think you need to do?"

I swallow. "I need to shake up the status quo."

"Exactly."

"But I can't do that without making people angry. Upset. Frustrated."

"Does a leader concern themselves with the hurt feelings of their soldiers? No, Karissa. This isn't personal. This is war. The sooner you all learn to put petty feelings aside, the sooner you'll be ready for what's coming. I trust you can manage that, but we shall see."

I nod. I know she's right. The feuds that run so deep in our little unit are so small in the scheme of things. Power and power plays won't matter if we wind up dead. And if we don't make it to the end, then what was it all for anyway? When the Inferiors are gone and we're rebuilding the world we always dreamed of, will we care about who took the top spot back in our training days?

"I'll do better. I will," I insist.

"Good. Very good. But I didn't just bring you here to talk about your performance. It's time for you to choose your Second," Captain Strauss says. "Have you thought about it?"

Of course I have. I've thought about it a thousand times. There are five people to choose from and each one of them has pros and cons. To me, the only one I can discount is Marcia. She's almost as much of an outsider as I am in the group, and certainly not skilled enough to be a Second. Then there's Ronan. A little quiet, but studious and skilled. He is one of the few that already listens to me when I give an order. Still, I can't picture him leading the group if something were to happen to me.

Then there's Minnie. She's not the worst choice I could make. She's not as skilled as some of the others, but she's popular in the group with a distinct ability to sway the people around her. Zach is in a similar boat, except he's maybe the best fighter we have too. Both of them would be good Seconds.

And then there's my brother.

There's no truly good choice. I know that I can't trust any of them. Their allegiances have been thrown off balance, but that doesn't make me their friend, or their ally. They will serve themselves, as they always have. I can understand that when it keeps them alive. But my Second has to be someone who won't stab me in the back the first chance they get.

That discounts every single one of them.

"It's a complicated matter. But I have thought a lot about it," I say. She raises an eyebrow.

"And?"

"And…I haven't come to my decision yet."

She folds her arms over her chest. "You understand that as Team Leader, you need to become more decisive, don't you?"

"I do. I understand that completely. But I also have to make the right decision. Right now, they don't recognize me as their leader. It's as you said, it won't happen overnight. Every decision I make seems to create further cracks in our foundations. I need to lead without hurting my cause further."

Captain Strauss sighs. "There's so much you're yet to understand. Power is a balance. You have a team of large personalities. Each one of them is potentially capable of overthrowing you."

"Perhaps not Marcia," I say. Captain Strauss almost cracks a smile.

"Perhaps not. But you know this already. You know that treading carefully has kept you level for now. You've walked the line between being authoritative but fair. That's why I always knew you'd make a good Team Leader. But in this case, fairness doesn't always matter. Elliott never played fair. You know that much. And it got him a long way in life. He got good at hiding the worst parts of himself, veiling them as power. Only when I exposed his flaws did the rest turn on him. If you want to remain in power, there are two things you have to do. Show them what you're made of - prove to them that you're every bit the Team Leader I know you can be. But you also need to be craftier. You have to show that you're the *only* choice. The only way to do that is to prove that no one else could stand where you stand. Now, think about that for a second. Does that help you in your decision of who to pick as your Second?"

I ponder her words. If I want to look good in my position, do I want my Second to look worse? Do I want their flaws to make me look like I'm better than I am? It seems wrong. But Captain Strauss is right. I can't play fair when the others aren't either. The problem with being surrounded by the best and brightest is that you can't afford a moment of weakness. You can't afford niceties if you want to be at the top. And the more I think about it, I do. I don't want to be squashed under Elliott's boot any longer. I want to show him that I can come back from the years of him pushing me down to the ground. But what's the phrase?

Keep your friends close and your enemies closer.

"I choose Elliott," I tell her. She raises her eyebrow.

"Interesting. Why, may I ask?"

"Because he's the opposite of me in every way. Cruel where I can be kind. Cunning while I'm trying to be fair. He's socially smart, able to manipulate others, but I'm smart in a different way. And I know that the smart thing to do is allow Elliott a semblance of power. Enough power to restore some of the fear the others had in him, to keep them in line. But not enough that he thinks he can take my place. I won't need to bully my team. He'll do it for me. They'll hate him. And they'll see me as the better option."

Captain Strauss' smile is real now. "I knew you'd figure it out. I think you've made a good decision. It might have been tempting to choose Zach, or even Minerva. But I think you've just proved to me that you've got what it takes. After we're done here, you'll need to announce your decision to the team. I expect they'll be surprised."

I know one person won't be. If anyone is going to expect this move, it's Elliott. Maybe it's a twin thing, but he's always known what I'll do next, always one step ahead of each decision I make. He'll see this coming a mile off. But if he understands why I'm doing it, that's when I'll really be in trouble. I guess that's something I'll just have to deal with when I come to it.

"Then it's settled. Elliott will be your Second. For better or for worse," Captain Strauss says, threading her fingers together. "And at the exact right time. I brought you here to warn you. Things are going to change soon, Karissa. You know what's coming. Our fight is only just beginning. You're young, but you're one of my best. You're strong and capable and I believe in you. I know things haven't been going well with your team…perhaps I should've stepped in sooner. But you'll turn it around. I'm telling you this because whatever you're going to do…you need to do it fast. You won't be sticking around here much longer. Do you understand?"

I nod solemnly. She's letting me know that we'll be going into the field soon. I've been trained my whole life for taking back the land which Captain Strauss grew up in. I always knew that one day, we would be sent to kill the Inferiors that infected the land. But I guess nothing prepares you for the reality of that.

We've been told ever since we started training that the Inferiors look like us, talk like us, live like us, but that we're different from them. Not just because of the X drug in our veins, or our superior intelligence, or our strength, but because they're barely human. They fight for scraps of the people we have become. They evolved differently from us and became a plague to our lands. They're the ones responsible for the overpopulation crisis, for the pollution of once beautiful lands, for leaving us no choice but to take back what is ours. There's millions of them and only a few of us. But Captain Strauss says that we can do this. That glory will be ours again. And I've always made a conscious choice to believe her, to have faith in her.

It feels different now. Ever since that day in Pain Endurance, when the X drug seemed to speak to me, to call out to me, I realized that my destiny has always been entwined with this war. It's showing me the way. Proving to me that I was always born to do this. I curl my hands into fists. I don't need faith.

I have power.

RILEY

I walk the city streets alone. I need to get away from the others for a while. Elianna isn't talking to me and Squid is coming down from the final high of last night. We have maybe enough money now to last us for a few days, to buy a few scraps of food that'll keep us going. But then what? I stuff my hands deep in my pocket. I'm clawing myself apart from the inside. Now that I've had time to really think about what we've lost, about what I've done to steal away the future from my friends, I'm filled with unimaginable guilt.

I thought I was doing the right thing. I thought I had control. But I got cocky, just like the rest. I let myself trust in a stranger and now I've got so much less than what I began with. The value of Bull's death has just dropped down to zero.

It's my fault. Elianna was right. I'm all of the things she's ever called me. Reckless. Selfish. Ruthless and dumb. I cringe away from myself, but there's no escaping who I am, *what* I am. I'm a death sentence I forced upon my friends.

The guilt is so painful it almost feels physical. I want to curl up in a ball to escape it. Why can I never get anything right? Why do I bulldoze my way through life and take down everyone with me? I'm a curse on everyone who meets me.

I stop short of the casino in a dark alley. I sink down among the dirt and the garbage, not caring that it stinks here and that I'm alone. I feel like I deserve to stew here and suffer. Wouldn't it be better for all of my friends if I just walked away from them now? I clench my fists in my lap, willing myself not to cry. I don't deserve to. But my breaths come hard and heavy. If I close my eyes, I see the anger on Elianna's face, the shame in Tiger's eyes, the sympathy in Squid's expression.

I'm a screw-up and they all know it.

I always knew I should have gone my way. I would've saved myself this kind of hurt as well as them. It may be self-inflicted, but it hurts all the same. I squeeze my eyes shut, but it doesn't go away. This is just another load to carry until the end of my days. Another shadow cast over my soul.

I'm a bloody waste of space.

I cry for a while until my throat is sliced up and raw. My body aches. I'm tired. Nothing feels good. I don't want to go back to my friends, but I also don't have the courage to walk away anymore. The big wide world has opened itself out to me and now it feels too big to handle when I've shrunk so small. I wish I'd just keep shrinking. Disappear entirely. I'd be doing everyone a favor.

"What are you doing down there in the filth, child?"

I look up with red raw eyes. It's the woman in the red coat. The overseer from the casino. She looks even more glorious out here in the dirty streets, her outfit a reminder that she lives in technicolor while the rest of us live in gray. She gets a little too close and I shudder back into the shadows. How dare she seek me out when she's the reason I'm like this? She cheated me out of my future.

"Leave me alone," I snarl, batting at the woman like an animal pawing at a human. She doesn't flinch in the slightest. Maybe if she knew what I'm capable of, maybe if she had seen what I can do, she might be more afraid of me. The way I am of myself.

"I think you need me," the woman says, bending down beside me. "I think I can give you another shot at getting things right. Don't you want to redeem yourself, for the sake of your friends?"

"What do you mean?"

"I have work available. The kind of work a girl like you would thrive at, I think."

I stare at her in horror. "Are you crazy? That's sick..."

"Not that kind of work, child. What do you take me for?" the woman says, her voice still soft as she scolds me. "No. Something brutal and cruel, yes...but I think you'll have a knack for it. Don't you want to hear what it is?"

I wrap my arms around myself. She's offering me paid work. Of course I want that. But I don't see how anyone can give me what I want and need. No one gives anything for cheap in this world. Whatever it is that she's offering me, it'll come at a price heavier to me than it is to her.

"I don't need anyone. Especially not you after you screwed me over," I mumble half-heartedly. The woman sighs.

"If only that were true. Why don't you listen to my proposition and then make a decision on what you need?" She leans in closer to me. "You'll die on these streets if you don't. You and your riff raff friends. I know your type. You lose so many times that every win makes you feel like you're untouchable. But you know better now, don't you? You learned the hard way. I watched you lose everything, little one. But I think you're a fighter. And I think I can give you a reason to fight."

"I don't want to fight anymore."

"No, I don't suppose you do. You're so young and so much has happened to you. But you've never known how to do anything else. You can still adapt, you can still change. I can show you the way. If you're willing to do something for me."

I laugh bitterly. "And there it is. You want to use me for something so you don't have to get your hands dirty, right? After you already ruined my life once over?"

The woman shrugs. "Aren't we all using someone for something?"

"I don't use people."

"Perhaps that's why you're the one shivering on the street and I'm the one with an offer you can't refuse. You either use people or prepare to be used." She sighs, touching my arm with a sympathetic smile. "Stop fighting it, little one. You know you don't have a choice."

I grit my teeth. She's right. Whatever she wants me to do, I'm going to do it. I'm taken back to years ago when I first looked Lion in the eye and accepted her offer to become a fighter in the Pits. I knew if I didn't, I would starve on the streets. I could've died on any given day from a stab wound or a blow to the head, but at least I would go down fighting for my life. That was the theory of it, at least.

But I don't want to do this anymore. I don't want to hurt other people. I never have. I don't want to use others as a stepping stone to one more day in hell.

And yet this isn't about me. It's about Squid and Tiger and Elianna. It's about giving them one more day after I took their chances away from them. It's about making up for my sins. I got so greedy, wanting win after win when I know that gambling is a losing game. Now we have nothing, and I'm the only one who can change that. I told myself I'd never do anything I didn't want to again. I was supposed to have bought my freedom the day I left the Pits with Bull's blood on my hands. But I walked out of one cage and into another. I'll never be the one with the power.

I might not be a winner, but I don't have to be a loser either.

"I'm in," I say softly. I may as well say *I'm yours.* Whatever it is she wants me to do, I'm at her mercy now. Refuse and I'll wind up dead. The woman offers me a beautiful, cruel smile.

"Of course you are."

She hands me a slip of paper and I take a look at it. I don't read well, but I know this is a name and an address. I glance back up at her.

"What do I do with this?"

"I think you know, child."

I swallow, sliding the piece of paper into my pocket. I wonder about who the person is, what they might have done. It doesn't matter anymore, really.

I'm going to end their life regardless.

"You'll be paid handsomely for your trouble. If you make it back and don't make too much of a mess," the woman says. "You'll have a room to share with your friends in the casino. You can work for me as long as you need to."

"And when I want to leave, you'll let me?"

The woman's eyes soften. "Yes. There will be no price for leaving here. So long as you do what I ask of you, you will be paid fairly."

"And if I die?"

"Then your money will go to your friends. And let them know there's plenty of work if they want it. Someone always wants someone else dead. Especially now."

I nod. This is it. The only way out. I rise to my feet, looking her right in the eyes.

"Show me to my room, then."

She raises an eyebrow at me as though she might scold me, but she doesn't. She puts a hand on my shoulder and guides me back toward the casino. Her touch is warm, but it makes me feel cold inside. It only reminds me of what she's going to make me do. I look up at her.

"How do you know I'll be able to do it?"

The woman smiles. "I know a killer when I see one."

RAVEN

It's the third day of Lark's imprisonment. He'll be let out today, but the moment can't come soon enough. I haven't been able to see or speak to him, but Kai has been left in charge of guarding his 'cell' so he's had more than one visit from me in the past few days.

"You need to chill out," Kai tells me as I approach him for my third visit of the morning. "Lark did a bad thing. This is a small price to pay for it. And surely he'll learn from his mistakes now that he's been made to suffer a little."

"For a fourteen year old you really do have some dark ideas. He was already going back on what he did…"

"Only because you told him he had to. This is the only way he'll learn. Three days without food? That's nothing compared to what some of us have been through."

"He's not like us. He's...fragile."

"Oh boo hoo. The poor little rich kid has a grumbly tummy…"

"Maybe this is our problem. Maybe we have to stop thinking of ourselves as 'us' and 'them.' You're treating him like he doesn't matter because he's led a different life to us."

"Don't tell me you've never judged someone because of their wealth or lack of it. Are you telling me you don't see

Logan differently after the life he's led? Besides, you don't see any of the poorer kids trying to steal stock."

"You know, you should probably remember that Lark's money *paid* for a lot of that stock. We'd be dead without him and his friends."

For once, Kai has nothing to say. He slumps in the chair he's sat in by the door to the 'cell', sulking. For the purpose of isolating Lark, the window looking into the room has been painted over with black paint, but as I peer through a slightly translucent gap in the glass, I can see him.

He's curled up in the corner of the room, hugging his knees. He doesn't look like the confident boy I'm used to seeing. His auburn hair is limp on his sweating forehead and his rumpled clothes seem out of place on him. He's lost weight very quickly. He's always had defined cheekbones, but now it looks as though his entire face is caving inward.

I don't care that the council deemed this a fitting punishment. Only Logan, June and I disagreed with the motion to imprison him, and others who have been caught since. It's *wrong*. We're living in a world where we can only rely on the people around us. How are we supposed to do that when guys like Roger want to inflict awful punishments at the drop of a hat?

Kai sighs as I continue to stare through the glass at Lark. "Look, he's going to be okay. You should be more worried about the food shortage. Everyone knows we're going to run out soon."

"We'll find more. We'll *make* more."

"You make it sound simple."

"It is simple, Kai. We'll find a way or we'll die. That's how it is. And I'm pretty sure what Lark did the other day proves that it won't be long before the rest of us resort to desperate measures to get what we want."

The thought terrifies me. How far will I go to survive? I want to believe I can remain good at heart, but in the past week, I've eaten a total of four meals. Not enough to sustain me properly for a day, let alone seven. My waist has always been slim, but now I can almost cup my hands around my entire middle. I'm wasting away. What would I do to put meat back on my bones a few weeks from now?

I've been lucky enough to never face true starvation before. Now, the likelihood of it happening seems to be more and more possible.

"Let me know when he's out, please," I tell Kai. Then I leave Lark behind for another day. If I had a choice, I wouldn't, but I have things to do today.

But tonight is a different story. Tonight is the next council meeting. And when I get there, I'm going to do everything I can to fight for Lark's case and any that might come after his.

This new world is cruel, but it doesn't mean we have to be.

"You need to eat something."

"I'm fine."

"No you're not. I just saw you go dizzy. You know why that's happening, right? It's a sign of the body shutting down."

I sigh. Logan and I are early to the meeting once again and he's already lecturing me. He tends to fuss over me like a mother hen. Endearing as it is, it's not helpful.

"Even if I wanted to, I don't have any, do I?"

Logan produces a cereal bar from his pocket and my eyes widen.

"No, Logan. Stealing? Really? After what happened to Lark?"

"I didn't steal it, I saved it from breakfast. I knew you'd need it more than me."

My hands are rested in fists on my knees, but he uncurls my fingers and places the cereal bar in my palm. A rush of warmth moves through me. It seems like my friends are always looking out for me. Logan. Lark, in his own selfish way. Wren...Wren was always the one to look out for me. I hang my head. I miss her so much it hurts.

I distract myself by breaking the bar in half.

"Eat it all, Raven. Jonah has eaten plenty today."

I don't say anything. I don't think Logan will ever understand my urge to protect Jonah so much. For years, he's been my only ray of sunshine. He's the only reason I keep going when things get tough. I could've given up years ago, the way my parents did. But Jonah kept me going, because I knew without me, he wouldn't stand a chance. Now, his life is in my hands more than ever and I'd do anything to protect him.

"If you don't take care of yourself, how can you take care of Jonah?" Logan asks me softly. It's like he knew exactly what I was thinking about. "Besides, things are looking up. We hit the jackpot today on our scavenger hunt. Roger really came through with a plan and now we don't need to worry so much."

I raise my eyebrow in surprise. "Really?"

Logan looks a little uncertain but he nods. "Yeah, I think things are going to be good now. Or better, at least. You can breathe a little."

I try to take that literally and draw in a deep breath before letting it out slowly. It feels good. I feel some tension leaving my shoulders. Logan smiles, his usual jokey self abandoned in favor of something else. Something sweeter. He nudges his knee against mine.

"I'm looking forward to you giving the council hell for what they did to Lark. So eat up."

He watches while I eat the entire thing. As I'm finishing up, Valeria arrives at the meeting. She nods to me solemnly. I stand up and walk over to her.

"Hey...can I count on your support today? I know you voted with the council last time…"

"My decision is final," Valeria says, folding her arms. "Life is tough. People need to follow the rules or face the consequences."

"I'm not saying there shouldn't be consequences...I'm saying it's too tough. Imprisonment and starvation? Come on, Valeria. I know you don't agree with that. What if one of your kids got caught stealing?"

Valeria's ears prick up. It's taken me this long to gather a little information about her, but now I know what drives her. I saw her a while back with a group of children. She was sending them off with Jonah to the classes that have been put on to help them get some form of education. I recognized some of the children from the area near the black market where there were rumors of a makeshift orphanage in place. After doing a little more digging, I found out that Valeria not only ran the orphanage herself, but had made a deal with the owner of the black market to support her kids. She'd come from money, but abandoned it for chasing down social justice. Her tattoo parlor made her enough money to keep herself and the kids afloat.

It seemed to me that someone fighting for socialist issues should be against starving someone. I pointed that out to Valeria, arguing my case for a whole five minutes before she sighed and looked at me.

"Look, Raven, this is a political situation at this point. It's not that I don't agree with you...but I have my reasons for the way my vote has swung. I've made up my mind."

I frown. I wonder what could possibly have made her abandon her own morals. She has to stand to gain something from it. The thought makes me angry. That's the problem here. Too many people looking out for themselves and not for one another.

I try to speak to a few others before the start of the meeting, trying to work on breaking them down to my way of thinking, but no one is interested. I know it's partly because I'm younger than the rest and they don't take me seriously, but they all seem to be on the defensive, claiming like Valeria to have motives of their own. I'm frustrated as we sit down to start the meeting. I'm buzzing with energy, but with no place to direct it to.

June starts the meeting, glancing in my direction with a sympathetic smile. "Okay, we're returning to the issue of crime and punishment first. Raven, the floor is yours."

I stand up, trying to ignore the fact that I feel a little dizzy still. I glance around the room.

"I want to ask you all to think again about how we treat those who have done wrong. We've been living in a society for a long time where the death penalty is handed out for petty crimes, but now that we're going independent from the government, we have the chance to start over. I would never suggest that we let people get away with crimes such as this, but starving people is where I draw the line."

"It's an eye for an eye, Raven," Roger responds cooly. "You steal food then you have food stolen from you."

"The isolation is more than enough of a punishment. Starvation can *kill.* And even then, I don't believe that isolation does anything to prevent crime happening again. It just gives people time with their thoughts to get riled up about the way they've been treated. Have any one of you been to take a look at Lark? He looks broken."

"Then perhaps it'll teach him not to do it again."

I ignore Roger, knowing that if I don't, I'll say something I regret and kill my case. "Our new society doesn't need us to be idle, sitting around and thinking about our mistakes. Instead of isolating people and starving them, why can't there be another way around this?"

"When have prison sentences ever worked in the past?" Logan chimes in. "History dictates that rehabilitation is much more useful. Don't take their humanity away. Give them something to work toward. Make everyone useful to the society they're trying to build," Logan says. I shiver at the comment. If we were more 'useful' to the government and their way of life, then they wouldn't be trying to wipe us from the world. But he's supporting my point so I nod.

"Yes. We have to choose to see the best in people or we're all going to fall apart. Why not have some kind of community service in place? Lark is already fighting for us on the wall every day, but maybe he could help scrub the kitchens, or lead a playgroup for the kids, or help out in the gardens."

"You think playtime is going to stop people from stealing? You must be mad," Roger says. "There's only one thing that deters people and that's fear. You do realize that crime rates have lowered massively since the government brought the death penalty back? Have some perspective, Raven. A few days alone in a room and less food is going to stop people doing things like that again. End of discussion."

I open my mouth to speak, but everyone in the room is already dismissing the topic. The second Roger declared the case closed, everyone began to shift in their seats, making it clear they are done with it too. I feel myself deflate. Not only has everyone turned their backs on my idea, but no one has even opened their mind to the possibility that I might be right. I glance around the room, wondering what could possibly make each of these people so loyal to Roger and his ideas.

"Well, plenty to think about," June says with a kind smile in my direction, but even she didn't back me up, which seems strange for a pacifist. I fold my arms and sit down, knowing that for today I've lost this battle.

"Roger wants to speak next," Ellis announces and everyone turns attentively to look at him. He smiles as he stands.

"Thank you, Ellis. I'd also like to thank everyone in the room for hearing me out. It's important that we listen to everyone's ideas."

Except if they're mine, apparently, I think bitterly. As though he's read my mind, he smiles in my direction and I feel my gut twist.

"Ellis and June should be commended for bringing this whole operation together. However, I think we need to think about taking this thing to the next level," Roger begins. "We're faced with a massive food crisis. We've got many mouths to feed and no means to do so. At least, we didn't, until we received a very generous donation…"

Roger glances at Logan with a warm smile and I feel my stomach drop. What have I missed here?

"I have connections to those who run the black market and they were willing to offer us very generous deals in exchange for two things; manpower and, of course, money. Logan here has supplied us with enough money to keep this deal going for an entire month. With this sizable donation, we will have that time to find new ways of becoming self-sufficient."

I stare at Logan in shock. He doesn't seem to realize that he's making a deal with the devil. When he looks at me and smiles, I know he's truly clueless to what this new alliance could mean for us all.

"I wasn't going to say anything," Logan whispers to me. "It's not a big deal. I know how important it is to you that this works out here...so I gave the last of my savings. I hope that's okay."

I can't find words to say to him. He thinks I'm bothered that he's now penniless like me, but that's not the issue at all. The issue is that he's funded whatever regime Roger has come up with. And though I'm sure he's far too smart to propose anything overly controversial right off the bat, I have a gut feeling that whatever comes next will be disastrous for us all.

But everyone is watching him like he's their guardian angel. Like he's given up everything for them and he's going to grow seeds of hope from the ground up. I wish I could believe that, but I don't trust him at all. What does he mean about the black market needing manpower? How can Logan's donation possibly last so long when he'd already given away the bulk of his money?

Roger is no doubt going to gloss over that.

"I have drawn up some plans for how we're going to make it through this thing," Roger says with a warm smile as he pushes a black folder into the center of the table. "This details work rotas for everyone, new plans for rationing to make the food last, and the selection of helpers who will be deployed in order to assist our new friends over at the black market. I know what some of you might be thinking. The black market is illegal. It implies that we can't trust the people in charge. But I like to believe I have good taste in people, and these are dear friends of mine. I can assure you we're safe in this deal, and it's going to give us a new shot at life."

It sounds too good to be true, and it probably is. I reach across the table. I want to be the first person to read these plans of his.

My reading level is very basic from my short time at school, but I can read enough to know I don't approve. The papers suggest longer working hours for those able to stay on their feet long enough, halved food portions and harsher punishments, including banishments from the safety of the building. It also puts Roger and his friends in a new position of power, putting them in charge of policing and punishment. I shake my head as Roger continues his speech. This isn't what we need. This is going to make everything worse.

It sounds to me like a dictatorship.

"What about education for the children?" I ask. "There's nothing in here about that. You've written that able-bodied children over the age of ten must work."

"We must all chip in if this is going to work. There's a lot to be done," Roger says calmly. He seems to believe he's being reasonable. "These children already know the concept of hardship. They will be happy knowing they're building toward a safer future for us."

I look around the room, looking for signs of discomfort on the faces of my fellow council members. I can't see any obvious signs of rebellion in their eyes. How can they think this is a good idea? This is exactly the life we grew up with. It's not a revolutionary idea to help build a community - it's falling back into old habits just with a new leader in place. I look at Valeria.

"Do you agree with this, Valeria? What about all those children you care for? Are you happy to put them to work?"

She doesn't meet my eyes and I know there's something I'm missing. This is the second time she's gone against what she would usually agree to.

"I have already discussed this matter with Roger," Valeria admits. "And for health reasons, they will be exempt from the workforce. I'm sure that this system will work well and won't exploit those who cannot work."

I narrow my eyes. *Health reasons.* Those kids are the healthiest out of anyone here. Valeria has given them a good life and lined their bellies. But then again, how can she refuse a better life for her children? How can she think of anyone else when she's got them to worry about?

It's selfish. It's cruel. But Roger knew exactly how to count on her support. I'm beginning to understand that now.

"But this is a democracy," Roger says with a warm smile. "Of course, we shall stay here and read this document together. Then we will vote for whether each of these ideas will be put into motion. Does that seem fair?"

Everyone in the room nods. Yes, it does sound fair. Or it *would* be fair if he hadn't already bought their votes. What else has he offered the people in this room? How many of them have been coerced into agreeing with his ideas?

Roger takes the document back from me and opens the first page. "Okay. The first item that we must vote on. All those in favor of increasing the working day by a further three hours per adult? I should remind you all that these extra hours will allow us to build a realistic foundation for our future. Let's vote. Raise your hand if you're in favor."

One by one, everyone in the room raises their hands. And that's when I realize the thing I've been missing for too long. While I've been chasing down social justice, Roger has been sneaking every member of the council into his back pocket. Even Logan has raised his hand in favor. He put his trust in Roger when he did the deal at the black market. And now, he's in debt to the man who will destroy us, so doesn't he have to vote in his favor?

I'm the only one who doesn't raise my hand. I'm not afraid of hard work; I can take it. But can the sick? Can the elderly? Can the children? He plans to push our physical and mental health to the limits, all for this supposedly brighter future. But it doesn't look bright to me. It's dimming with every passing moment.

Am I crazy to think Roger has something other than good intentions for us when he seems intent on throwing us into the depths of hell?

EPILOGUE

Captain Strauss approached the plane with her hands threaded behind her back, admiring the scene before her. Her plans were finally coming to fruition. So many years of being shunted into the darkness. And now she was being given an opportunity to start over, to give her people a new lease of life.

Phase two would take care of that.

The first wave of soldiers would be shipped off in less than an hour. They were tasked with infiltrating the cities, getting a lay of the land for the next wave of soldiers that would be following them shortly. It was a dangerous mission. Strauss had no doubt that many of her soldiers wouldn't make it. But that had never been her concern. She had trained these young people to live and die for their right to freedom. They would die knowing that they ranked higher than the people who sought to kill them. And if they made it through, they would be among the new Elite race.

Or some of them would be, at least.

As Captain Strauss approached the plane, she saw one of her best and brightest stood by, assembling her team for action. Team Seven were her highest performing set of rookies in a long time. There was no time to send them on to Advanced Training, but she knew it wouldn't matter. They were led by Adelaide, who at seventeen was already better than most of the soldiers under Strauss' command. Strauss was always wary of girls like Adelaide. She stood out from the crowd. Small and slight, but strong and intelligent. These were the girls born to rival her and the position she had worked so hard for. But Strauss had taken measures to ensure she wouldn't be replaced. Not by Adelaide, or Karissa, or any of the other young women who sought to outdo her. They would not take their place among the Elites. Someday, and someday soon, the talent that was housed within them would burn a hole right through them.

Adelaide turned when she saw Captain Strauss approach and saluted. Strauss smiled. *I trained them well.*

"At ease. There will be no formalities among us any longer," she said, offering her hand for Adelaide to shake. "You and your team are doing me proud."

A faint blush tainted Adelaide's cheeks. "Thank you, Captain. I am honored to serve my country. This is what I've waited my entire life for."

Poor girl. Strauss knew from the sincerity in Adelaide's voice that she had done her job far too well. Adelaide truly believed there was nothing more to life than beating the opposition down, to restoring the balance, to killing Inferiors and coming out on top. Not that it mattered. Adelaide would be gone by the time the new world came into order. She was a ticking time bomb, whether she knew it or not. Captain Strauss eyed her up. She was already starting to look worn down. Bloodshot eyes, thin, waxy skin. Was she imagining the gauntness in her cheeks, the thinning of her hair?

The Y drug would make her unstoppable.

And then it would break her down entirely.

"How do you feel?" Strauss asked Adelaide quietly. Adelaide blinked.

"Honestly? Never better."

"Still having the strange dreams?"

Adelaide swallowed. "Yes. But the doctor says it's nothing out of the ordinary. Just teenage hormones. An overactive imagination, perhaps."

"What about the euphoria? The grandiose thoughts?"

Adelaide smiled. "I don't know. Perhaps I'm just excited for what's to come."

"Yes, of course. Just don't allow it to interfere with your goals, okay?"

Adelaide blinked. "I would never."

"Then there's no issue, is there? Do you and your team have enough supplies of the X drug?"

"Yes, I've checked over their packs. Enough to last for a month. Until the next phase when we can get more."

"Excellent. Then I suppose there's nothing more to do. You can be on your way."

Adelaide reached hopefully for Strauss' hand again and she shook it willingly. This would be the last time she would see this perfect young woman. She had no reason for animosity toward her any longer.

"Thank you, Captain. For everything," Adelaide whispered.

"No," Captain Strauss said with a smile. "Thank *you*. For your sacrifices."

TO BE CONTINUED…

BOOK 3: GREED

COMING 8TH OCTOBER 2023

ABOUT THE AUTHOR

HAYLEY ANDERTON is a full time ghostwriter and the author of the YA LGBT romance novel, Double Bluff. She is also the co-author of the Kindle Unlimited series, Apocalypse. When she's not writing she loves to bake and hang out with fluffy friends. For editing services and business enquiries, she can be contacted at hayleyandertonbusiness@gmail.com.

Instagram: @hayley_a_writes
Twitter: @handerton96
Wattpad: @hazzer123

If you enjoyed this novel, please consider reviewing it on Amazon and Goodreads! Reviews can make or break an indie author's career, so any thoughts you have are much appreciated!

Printed in Great Britain
by Amazon